I0670580

Perfect Stats

WINNING HER

AMBER MALLOY

Winning Her
ISBN # 978-1-83943-882-0
©Copyright Amber Malloy 2020
Cover Art by Louisa Maggio ©Copyright April 2020
Interior text design by Claire Siemaszkiewicz
Totally Bound Publishing

WINNING HER

Dedication

To Lisa, Thanks for all the crazy faces.
Who knows where this story would have gone
without them!

Prologue

Millions of people watched the battle-scarred warriors smash their bodies to bloody pulps. They cheered from the comfort of their homes, bars and the sidelines of the football field. The force of one hit from the opposition was akin to a small-impact car collision. Bane Carter kept all this in mind as he beat back the scream of pain that clawed its way from the depths of his soul.

"Tell me this isn't happening," the defensive coach complained as he adjusted the mouthpiece to his headset and mumbled into the microphone.

For the foul committed against Bane, the referee gave their opponents a technical.

"Fuck!" he yelled.

Bane tried to fight through the intense hurt to do an internal check. Ribs bruised or broken, ankle sprained or fractured—he simply didn't know. The overwhelming agony attacked every muscle in his body and squeezed. Vomiting the pain away might offer him a bit of relief but for how long? Bane wanted — no, needed — someone to knock him unconscious.

"X-rays are the only way we'll know how extensive the damage is," the EMT said. Or was it the physical trainer?

Shit! Bane couldn't even think straight.

Five minutes until halftime and the Bobcats were up by two piddly little points — not much, but enough to get them into the playoffs. The opposition was known for coming back strong in the fourth quarter. Considering that they'd taken out most of his team's defensive line, odds were suddenly in their favor.

"Tell me it's not that bad. Without Beast here, we're out of the playoffs," the coach whined.

"Like I said, we can't tell until — "

"Yeah, yeah, X-rays," the coach interrupted him.

"One… Two…"

"No, no, no," Bane begged. "*Argh*!" As the paramedics picked up the sides of the gurney, his stomach rolled in waves of agony. He needed a shot of Hennessy, bourbon — or anything — for the pain.

"One of our physical trainers will be coming with you, Carter. Oh, hey!" He touched the side of his head to listen to his earpiece. "Security is bringing Dahl. Driver, hold up." The coach hit the sidewall of the ambulance to stop them.

"No," Bane hissed. "Just go."

"But she's like ten seconds away. We can wait — "

"Go! I said *go*!" He might not have had too many coherent thoughts past the pain, but Bane knew without a shadow of a doubt that he couldn't let his beyond-beautiful wife into the ambulance.

Dahl's father's recent diagnosis of Parkinson's disease had sent her reeling. He couldn't trust her not to mention the actual number of concussions he'd

8

received, which was well over the protocol limit. He knew she would tell the extent of his injuries to the doctors and that would mean no more football—career over.

Bane truly loved Dahl more than anything or anyone in the world, but football had been his life since the age of thirteen. He refused to choose between the woman of his dreams and the career he'd always wanted.

"Oh, okay." The coach frowned then shut the door to the ambulance and turned toward Dahl.

The small window allowed him to see her stop and listen to whatever lame excuse the man wove. While Dahl shoved the silky tendrils of her hair away from her heart-shaped face, she tilted her head to the side. Unfortunately, he knew that look. Tears simply weren't in Dahl Baby Hamilton's emotional toolbox.

Instead, unmitigated honey-badger rage would rear up from out of nowhere. For a split second he was worried about his coach's well-being.

Another wave of pain racked his soul. "What's the hold up? Let's go," he groaned. Bane didn't want to be a witness to her reaction. If he was brought into court, he would hate to have to testify against her. However, there was no mistaking the dead-eyed stare she pinned him with as the ambulance pulled off.

This isn't a big deal. He was hurt, after all. She shouldn't be too mad at him... *Right?*

Chapter One

Twelve years later…

From the minute Dahl Hamilton had stepped into First Down's kitchen, she'd worked nonstop. Tasked with fixing the failing restaurant, she'd barely seen the inside of her fabulous downtown loft, let alone her sweet, sweet bed. After having labored in the kitchen for more than two months, she was finally seeing all her hard work paying off.

The Chicago Tribune and *Sun-Times*, among other publications, had awarded First Down stellar reviews. Since the papers had hit the newsstands, customer attendance had shot up by more than fifty percent. If everything worked out, she could leave before autumn to work on more personal projects.

As Dahl topped off the dessert plate with her 'D' embellishment, the incessant ringing of someone's cell caught her attention. That was a definite no-no in the kitchen. She requested the name of the offender.

"Marco!" the kitchen staff of twenty screamed in unison.

"You know the deal." Before Dahl plated one perfect, mouth-watering slice of tiramisu cake, she pointed at the fine jar. The funds went toward their holiday festivities. At this rate, First Down's Christmas party would be one for the history books.

"Smaller cuts," she advised her assistant at the next station over. The restaurant had a full house, so the staff needed to move fast to keep up. During all the chaos, she found time to teach the newbies a trick or two. "Use your wrist. No one wants to bite a chunk of onion on their first date."

Breaking her signature snicker-cookie in half, she placed it on top of the whipped cream ruffle.

"Hello, Dolly. I wanted to make changes to the menu." The office manager, Beth, breezed into the kitchen. "Can we talk out back?"

She slapped the woman's hand away before she could grab the leftover half of the cookie. "It's just 'Dahl'...and no." She'd taken this consulting gig to help out her cousin. Nothing in the fine print read that she had to take orders from their idiot manager.

"We can't go outside—or we can't change the menu?" she asked in that snooty, superior tone.

Dahl handed the dessert off to the server and faced Beth. "To both... It's no to both."

"But Melanie told me to tell you—" Dahl held up her hand to kill the twit's whining. She didn't have the time. Instead, she went back to the orders. Soon the team would be able to catch their own mistakes. Busy checking the tickets against the meals, she missed the hush that fell over the kitchen. The usual clanging of pots and silly banter flipped into a strange vacuum of silence.

"Why are you here?" His deep, steely voice sent tingles up her spine. Dahl gazed at the six-foot-seven wall of well-dressed, muscled sexy.

Against her will, she smiled. "Hi," she said.

Better looking than any action star, Bane's good genes were wasted on football, in Dahl's opinion. He should have gotten out years ago, but nope… *Little boys grow up to be big men with dreams that become everyone else's nightmares.*

"Once again, why are you here?" Bane Carter asked. Her ex-husband smelled amazing.

"That's a loaded question, Mr. Carter. I'm going to need an assist."

"What?"

"Maybe rephrase…" She wiped her hands on her apron and leaned against the counter. "Are you asking why am I in Chicago, why am I in the restaurant or why am I still breathing? The throbbing vein in the middle of your forehead is screaming that it's the latter."

Stepping closer, he filled in the space between them. "Pick one through three," he growled.

Unable to hide her nerves, she laughed. The attack of childish giggles overwhelmed her. It often happened at the most inopportune times and she couldn't help it. His handsome face went blank before he abruptly turned and walked away. As general manager for the Mavericks football team, Bane probably didn't get challenged very often — or most likely ever.

He turned and left, as quickly as he'd come. Dahl sighed. After all these years, she'd thought she was over him. "Okay, everyone, back to work!"

"Was that Bane Win—?"

"Yep," she cut off her sous chef in an effort to deter any more questions.

"Did anyone notice how fast Bad-management Beth dipped out when he came in?"

The team laughed — but Dahl didn't join them.

* * * *

Tamping down the little bit of patience he had left, Bane stared out of the window of his cousin's office. It was chilly but not freezing, and occasional foot traffic went by.

Earlier that afternoon he'd attended a press conference that had circled the drain at an alarming rate. The police protest had taken center stage. The media wanted answers, but it had become clear they weren't interested in the truth.

As the only general manager of color in the league, Bane had been expected to field all the questions, no matter how ridiculous. Having been born to African-American military parents made him the resident professor on all things race related. Flipping the reporters' vague answers allowed him to keep the owners off his back.

"If you would just let me talk — " his cousin, Trey Carter, started. Bane had introduced Trey to Dahl's cousin Melanie at their engagement party. The two had ended up boning that same night in the restaurant's coatroom and they'd been happily stupid ever since.

"You've had plenty of time to tell me you invited Dahl into the restaurant to help ou before now. Either you meet my new terms or I'm pulling my investment out of it." He didn't do family handouts. *Nobody* got a free ride.

Maybe he should have visited First Down more than twice in the two years since it had opened. However, his schedule wasn't flexible.

13

"It's not that simple. I needed her to—"

Done with the conversation, he headed to the door. Out of all people, his cousin should have known better than to bring Dahl anywhere near him. The lack of loyalty pissed him off. "Backing you was already a stretch—and this proves it." He grabbed the doorknob.

"Chasing after a ball and getting hit in the head isn't for everyone, I guess."

Bane glanced over his shoulder at Trey. Years ago, his cousin had tried out for the league and failed. Big hopes and no effort had forced him to fall short time and time again. No matter how much he wanted to blame all this on him, Bane knew the fool only followed his shallow wife's lead.

Melanie wanted all the finer things in life but refused to put in the work. Bane regretted the day he'd introduced them. Trey might have been a better person if they'd never met.

"I've got three kids mourning their parents' deaths and one baby who has no clue what's going on. Taking blows to the head didn't cause any of that."

"Look, man... I told you we would help, but you haven't asked us—"

"I haven't seen you at my house since the memorial." Bane cut his bullshit short.

"Well, the restaurant takes a lot of our time, and—"

"Save it," Bane growled. "I doubt First Down needs more than one person to run it into the ground."

"It's not that bad." Trey pouted like a freaking kid.

"Yeah, nothing ever is with you. Look... Cady only eats chicken nuggets and the other kids don't know what a vegetable even looks like." He opened the door. "Have Dahl at my house, ready to cook, or I'm pulling every dime out of this place, plus interest."

"Hey, what happened to the nanny?"

14

Bane walked out of the door. For years he had steered clear of his family. Initially, he'd given small investments here and there but nothing too substantial. Nevertheless, after his brother's death, he'd wanted to fix everything.

That turned out to be an even bigger mistake than I could ever have imagined.

Chapter Two

The three-story mansion loomed in front of her. Dahl sat in her truck, contemplating her next move. A simple family favor had turned into a nightmare straight out of *The Twilight Zone*. In no uncertain terms would she ever make that mistake again.

She hit the SUV's Bluetooth to listen to her voicemail.

"Hey, girl, I know you're mad, but once this blows over, you'll see we had no choice. If Bane pulls out of the restaurant, we'll lose everything. Anyway, thanks. And…well, I hate to ask you this now, but do you know where the vendor list is? There's a fish guy here that wants a check and Beth doesn't know—" Dahl deleted Melanie's voicemail.

The title 'spoiled princess' didn't do her cousin justice. In childhood, it might have been an adorable personality flaw, but left unchecked, it had sadly turned her into a terrible disease named S.A.S.—shitty adult syndrome.

When Dahl had been all set to pack her stuff and leave, her cousin had begged her to stay. Of course, her cooperation had come with strings attached that Melanie and her husband simply couldn't afford.

As a world-renowned chef with several cookbooks under her belt, Dahl had her own television series consulting and rehabilitating restaurants. If First Down failed, it would reflect badly on her brand, which left her with no choice but to accept Bane's ridiculous ultimatum. Against her better judgment, she got out of her truck and walked up to the front porch.

She pushed the doorbell of the brown brick Tudor-style mansion. After waiting several minutes, Dahl was ready to give up. Before she hightailed it back to her truck, someone finally opened the door.

"Down here."

Dahl took a step forward to see the curly-haired pixie who could barely touch the big brass knob.

"Are you supposed to be answering the door?" Dahl asked with a chuckle. As she was stepping inside the enormous house, the little girl moved an unruly curl out of her face.

"No, but you kept ringing."

"Fair enough. Is there an adult around?"

The pixie shook her head. "Chelle went to the store but hasn't come back. Jarin is in his room, and there's my big sissy, Alana. I don't know where she went."

Dahl couldn't help but notice the air of listlessness that clung to the youngster. "My name's Dahl." She lowered herself down to the kid's level.

"Like a dolly?" Her big brown eyes opened wide.

"Yeah, just spelled different. What's yours?"

"Cady."

"Are you hungry, Cady?"

The brown-haired munchkin nodded her head.

"Great." Dahl stood up and offered the little girl her hand. "Can you show me the kitchen?"

"Yes."

"Do me a favor, kid." She let Cady lead her toward the back of the house. "Don't answer the door anymore."

"What if someone is there?"

"Consider it the beginning buzzer for a game of hide and go seek. If you answer, then you're automatically it. Okay?"

"Okay," Cady said.

"So what do you like to eat?"

"Chik'n nuggets."

Dahl laughed. The only dietary instructions she'd received from Bane had explicitly stated not to make chicken nuggets, *ever*.

* * * *

Bane got home late. Contract negations weren't going his way. They were stuck with a nightmare of a quarterback and the team needed to get rid of him... ASAP.

Attacked by a crazy ball of kiddie giggles once he walked in the door, he chuckled. "Uncle Bane!" It was well past the time for the little one to be in bed, but he let Cady hug his leg. He walked through the kitchen with a four-year-old bolt of energy attached to him.

"Chelle said I could wait up for you."

"What else did she say?" Chelle, his nanny, was a C-minus babysitter who was steadily dropping to D fast. He'd had the hardest time finding someone better. After his brother Devon and wife Isabella's deaths, he'd searched for a more appropriate place for the kids to live. No one wanted all four of them, and Bane wouldn't allow them to be separated.

Alana, the oldest, was typing away on her phone but looked up to say, "She said that chef is a bust. She didn't actually cook. You should think about hiring someone else."

He sighed. Bane waited for more of her word vomit, told from the perspective of one of the most narcissistic creatures on Earth—a teenager—and he was positive that the picture she was drawing didn't resemble anything close to the truth. The last thing he wanted to deal with was a five-foot, four-inch bundle of teenage crazy.

"So, yeah, she basically came and did nothing," Alana said.

"She didn't cook anything, nothing at all?" he asked. "You didn't eat?"

After grabbing Dahl's list off the fridge, he opened the door and went for a beer then twisted off the top.

The pretty girl shifted her weight from foot to foot before she finally looked up. "Well, I ate, but she didn't make what I wanted."

"And you think I should fire her for that?"

Alana shoved her nose into the air. "If she doesn't do what we want, then..." For a fleeting moment he wondered if hormones had created this entitled psycho—or perhaps the sudden change in her environment had encouraged all her inner demons to fly out.

"Considering you barely make your own bed, I'm not going to defer to you for hiring or firing decisions. However, if at any point you would like to perform a chore or two, we'll revisit this conversation."

"Y-you..." she stuttered.

Having been on the receiving end of more than one tantrum, he took a healthy swig and waited.

19

"Never listen to me." Her voice hit an irritating screech.

Bane waved his fingers in the motion of a symphony conductor. "Got to tell you, Alana. This is becoming my favorite song."

"*Argggh*!" she screamed.

"Wait." He tried to hide his amusement behind his beer bottle. "What did she cook—but not really cook?"

"Seggeti," Cady answered. Bane glanced down at the four-year-old, almost forgetting she was still attached to his leg.

"What am I, three?" His eldest niece stomped off.

"Did you like it?" he asked the little one, limping to the chef's island.

"Almost better than Mommy's." Cady smiled up at him.

He ruffled the kid's unruly mop of curls and took another hit of his Miller's. Nearly forgetting about Dahl's note, he glanced down at her artsy cursive. *She knows I hate cursive. She does this shit on purpose.*

Talked to the Perdue company about the strict no-nugget ban introduced into the Carter household. They are definitely not happy about the actions of one Winston Bane Carter. Cady's hard-core addiction can't be solved by the cold turkey approach. They suggest a slow and easy program, where maybe three to four nuggets are allowed at lunch. If their request is denied, they will seek further assistance from Foghorn J. Leghorn. Yes, it is weird that a Brahma chicken oversees the consummation of other chickens, but it's a dog eat dog world. Teehee, that's a little joke from the poultry community.

Sincerely,
Dahl Baby Hamilton.

Bane groaned. A woman from his past that he had never wanted to let go of took center stage in his mind. Flashes of their relationship swam around in the frontal cortex of his brain, moving everything else out of the way. The day they'd broken up, he'd prayed that he'd never see her again. On the bright side, she'd persuaded Cady to eat something other than garbage, which was sort of a win. He hoped to survive this beautiful intrusion.

* * * *

As days passed, Dahl had managed to navigate between First Down and the Carter household without any hiccups. She usually arrived at Bane's after everyone had already left in the morning then hit the restaurant before the dinner rush. There had been no major catastrophes thus far, but she didn't hold out hope that it would stay that way.

Considering that she hadn't seen a hint of Bane or the nanny, she figured she'd walked straight into a *Home Alone* situation. Since their last meeting had been nothing less than brutal, she didn't mind that the big man had kept his distance. The kids, on the other hand, were a whole different animal. At this point, she doubted even the mere existence of a nanny. Dahl expected to see Big Foot or the Loch Ness monster first.

"Is this good?" Cady asked.

Dahl inspected the cookie balls she was rolling in her palm. "Perfect. When you're done, we'll pop them in the oven." To keep the sweet girl busy, she provided her with different kitchen duties.

"Can I make a request?" Alana asked. She sauntered into the kitchen without looking away from her phone. "Or will we be eating off the kid's menu once again?"

Dahl ignored her. She didn't have time for her funky attitude.

"Hello?" Alana barked.

"Talk to me when you're done with your phone."

"Why can't you just answer the question?"

The teenage whine nearly made her knock the cell out of the girl's hand. Instead, Dahl finished cutting the potatoes into steak fries. After sprinkling them with ranch dressing rub, she loaded the pan into the industrial oven.

Bane's kitchen had all the bells and whistles. It was simply a chef's dream.

"Why can't you put down your phone?" The school district was off for the last few days. Dahl had counted on a showdown with Alana—but not this soon.

"You work for me!" she hollered. Rage contorted her young face. If Dahl actually needed this job, little-bit's anger might have intimidated her.

"Don't you scream at my Dolly," Cady yelled at her sister.

"Shut up!"

Tired of the girl's crap, Dahl pointed at the doorway but the teen didn't move. Instead, she folded her arms and stared Alana down. "That means walk," she snapped at the bratty girl. "Do one more row, sweetie, then we'll stick those in the oven." Dahl rubbed the curly-haired munchkin's head on her way past. Cady stuck her tongue out at her sister, the four-year-old's equivalent of the middle finger.

"Look... I don't do special orders. If you want something specific, then fix your mouth to ask nicely... and still, I can't guarantee it," she said, once they'd made it far enough away from her sister's ears. "Also, and this is important, I *don't* work for you."

"Ah, but you work for my uncle, and that means—"

22

Low on time, Dahl cut her entitled mess off with a snort. "Ten bucks says you told on me." The pretty teen's gaze slid away from hers. "And what did he say when you did?"

"Well, if I"—she tucked one of her black ringlets behind her ear—"tell on you again, then..." She swallowed.

The evil witch cackle erupted from Dahl's soul and fed off of the kid's naïveté. "Honey, you're going to need to stick to boys, lip gloss and calculus, because this here is"—she gestured above her head with a whistle—"way above your pay grade. Listen... You've been through a hell of a tragedy, but you're going to have to sort out your feelings in a more productive manner than this."

Biting her lower lip, the teenager took a step back. "What do you know about it?" Her voice quivered.

"I know about high school and being different. If you don't fight your way to the surface, you sink." A slight pink blush attacked Alana's mocha skin. After dealing with a ton of waitstaff over the years, Dahl no longer bothered to use the 'easy' button. "Just because you're the new girl doesn't mean you get to hide behind anger and a nasty attitude. Believe me... What you put out there is what you're going to get back."

"Dolly, I'm done," Cady called.

"Think about it." She left the kid in the hallway. Between playing referee and food prep work for the week, she only had half the time to get the meals made for the next couple of days.

"Good job, kiddo." She high-fived Cady and grabbed the pan on her way past. "We'll just put them in here." Dahl opened the oven and slid the cookies onto the lower rack.

"Do I know you?" a voice asked.

She peered over her shoulder at an older woman, who had snuck into the room.

"Not that I'm aware of." She shut the oven door and turned around to greet her. "Dahl, the temporary chef."

"Ester. House manager for a million years and now sometimes a baby nurse, but not at night. Thankfully, he hired someone for that." After she shrugged into her coat, she held out her hand. "I'm surprised we haven't bumped into each other before now. This house is pretty big, though, and I don't work full time or even every day." Reaching over the chef's island, Dahl took the statuesque woman's hand into hers. It was cold to the touch, and Dahl resisted the urge to ask about her health.

Discolored patches changed the pallor of the woman's skin, so Dahl automatically wondered if the house manager was sick. "It seems everyone around here has full schedules," Dahl noted.

"But I've seen you before." Ester shook her finger. "I don't forget faces."

Dahl simply smiled. Unless Ester had The Culinary Channel on repeat, she doubted they'd ever met. "Is there anything special you want me to make?" She knew her question leaned toward intrusive, but she'd worked with clients who had dietary restrictions in the past. The information would help for food prep.

"No, no, honey, I'm fine. Just make sure these babies get what they need." Ester squeezed Cady's cookie-dough-covered cheeks in her hand. Elbow-deep in the bowl, the girl was scraping the sides. "Just a heads-up… I'm leaving early. The night nurse should be here any moment now, but in case she's late…" She placed a baby monitor on the counter.

"What about the nanny?" Dahl asked.

Ester swiveled her head from side to side. "Have you seen her? Because I certainly haven't."

"Not even her ghostly impression," Dahl admitted.

The older woman waved her hand. "Get used to it, my dear. I've told Bane a thousand times, but..." She drifted off. "Oh well, have a good night."

"Let me know if there's something special you would like. The kids aren't the only ones who need to eat."

Ester paused at the back door with her hand on the knob. "Are you any good at Cajun?"

"The best."

"I'll be that judge of that, young lady. Oh, I almost forgot." Ester dug into her pocket and pulled out a piece of paper. "This was on the fridge. I didn't want one of the kids to accidentally move it."

While sliding the bowl away from Cady's little clutches, Dahl accepted the note. "Hey!" the little girl protested. She was a virtual cookie mess and it would take forever for Dahl to un-sticky the kid.

"Étouffée... Can we start there?" Ester asked her. Dahl nodded with a slight smile and opened the folded paper. Bane's hard, serial-killer scrawl shot her into a time warp back to a time where they actually liked each other.

First, I would like to commend all parties involved that made it possible for Cady to eat real food. As for the threats made by one Foghorn Leghorn, justice will be meted out swiftly. If this includes teaming up with Elmer Fudd, then so be it. Who among us doesn't like fricasseed chicken? Keep up the good work.
Sincerely,
Bane Carter.

Chapter Three

Exhausted, Dahl stepped into the Hotel Peninsula's lobby with its elegant high ceilings and chandeliers. As the CNN producer waved at her, she shoved her loose curls away from her face and walked into the dining room.

"Sorry I'm late." She slid into the seat next to him. "It's been a rough couple of weeks."

The producer for her first cooking show, Jeff Shaffer, knew his way around a tight budget. He'd taken their mess of a program on a test run for the Cooking Network and landed them a full season. After that, they had scored a second show on the Travel Channel.

For five consecutive years, her team had managed to win the Nielsen ratings before her numbers had dropped. The network wanted to retool the show, providing it with a facelift. Dahl had vetoed anything trendy and taken a much-needed break.

"Not a prob. I haven't been waiting long. You look great, by the way." She snorted at his compliment. He had that California schmoozing thing down to a science. "No, really, I don't know what you're doing."

Dahl reached for the water and took a sip. She'd been pushed to write another cookbook by her team, so she figured she would field offers for another show while she played with recipes.

"We want a documentary-type program that could compete with *Parts Unknown*."

"Sounds good, but knock-offs don't generally work."

"You've got me there. We want to make this one about American history, with the common thread being types of food that were born out of tragedy."

"Are we researching food or trying to win an Emmy for overdramatic shit?"

"I forgot how direct you can be." Jeff chuckled.

The vibration from her purse pulled her attention. "Sorry," Dahl apologized. "I thought I'd turned it off." She dug into her bag, which hung over the back of her chair. With every intention of silencing it, something made her slide the tab to the right instead.

"Hey, Cady, what's going on?" She held up her finger to Jeff.

"Jarin ate all my food for the week," the little girl blubbered out. "He had his friends over an-and Chelle isn't here for me to tell and Alana won't give me any nick'n nuggets."

"Okay, I'll see what I can do." She threw Jeff a tense smile, positive he could hear the little girl's high-pitched cry over the phone.

"Hurry, okay?" She hiccupped.

She'd provided Cady her number in case of an emergency and had severely underestimated the kid's propensity for dramatics. Apparently the lack of nuggets had ranked very high on the four-year-old's list.

"Sorry."

"No problem. Kid emergencies? I know how that goes."

"More like a food emergency. How about we do a rain check?" Dahl slipped her purse over her shoulder, already considering the meeting over.

"Sure," he agreed, a little defeated.

"With a different pitch, right? Because that one super sucked."

"Oh." Jeff's lips turned down into a slight pout, a pathetic sight to witness from a grown man. Needless to say, she'd seen it too many times to count. Dahl headed out of the swanky restaurant's door. She didn't want to get stuck soothing his wounded ego.

* * * *

Bane sat in the conference room with the Mavericks' coach and owner. They went through their roster, looking to make at least three more cuts before camp. His wish list included Shawn Mathers, but everyone loved the entitled prick.

"Right now, we're looking at guys with half the talent. We can't afford to let him go," the coach said. The man had been complicit in allowing the quarterback's many transgressions to slide, so Bane had a hard time taking him seriously.

"Mr. Carter, your nanny is here to see you."

"Nanny, huh? Is that a euphemism for something else?" The owner, Coop Ranger, laughed. The old man let out an ancient cough, while their brown-nosing coach joined him.

"No. I got custody of my brother's kids when he died. She's actually just the nanny." He hit the button on the intercom. "Show her into my office." Bane got up, wondering what the hell had happened.

"With all this 'Me Too' mess going on, I'd be careful if I were you, son."

"Give me five," he told the men, earning a much-needed break from the freakin' *Dukes of Hazzard* Sheriff Roscoe and Cooter act.

The Ranger family owned several sports franchises. They were conservative to the core, and Bane knew they considered him a pity hire because of the color of his skin. No matter how high he brought up the team's rankings, they still saw him as their 'affirmative action' baby.

A couple of seasons back, the *Sun Times* had written a hit piece about the family's lack of diversity in their sports programs. After they had been publicly shamed, he had become their first African-American GM.

Bane walked a fine line. Any little stumble and he would be out. That was why he wanted to get rid of Mathers—sooner rather than later. The guy was one big, ticking time bomb of trouble, ready to detonate.

Afraid that Chelle, his nanny, had trekked from the house to the arena in another shitty attempt at seduction, Bane opened his office door. However, his heart pounded an extra beat at the sight of Dahl Baby Hamilton.

As she shot him a heated glare, soft curls fell onto her lovely face. Jeans, a tank top and an expensive tailored leather jacket molded to her tight body. They were basic clothes on anyone else, but they appeared action-movie sexy on her—a far cry from the chef's apron she usually wore. He had to tear his eyes away to avoid drooling. After all these years, he had hoped she looked like crap. *Fat freaking chance.*

"It's been what, three weeks since you blackmailed me into cooking for your family?"

"No one twisted your arm, Dahl." He stared out the floor-to-ceiling window and surveyed the football field, wishing she would vanish, in much the same way she had all those years ago.

"If Trey and Melanie's place— Sorry." She smirked in that needling way that drove him crazy. "I meant that if *your* restaurant goes under, my reputation is on the line."

"Whose fault is that? I didn't ask you to save those clout-chasing idiots. The current predicament you find yourself in is not my problem."

Bane had forgotten that Dahl never shrank away from a fight. A growl here or a hiss there could easily get anyone off his back. Instead, she stepped closer.

"Well, Bane Carter, let me share all *your* problems." The menacing cadence of her already-smoky voice spiked his blood pressure. "Cady called me crying about the food I prepared in advance because Jarin, who never comes out of his room, has eaten all of it." She held up one finger on her hand. "Those kids need counseling, but mainly Alana, who is about to have the biggest hormone explosion of any teenager I've ever met." She put a second finger up.

"Are you done?"

"Not even close," she told him with way more glee than the moment deserved. "I'm pretty sure your office-slash-baby nurse has some kind of medical condition that she is keeping from you, but don't quote me on that one." That announcement prompted her to put a third finger in the air.

"What?" Ester was the closest thing he'd ever had to a mother. The thought of her hiding an illness made his chest tighten. "How do you know?"

"The better question," she shot back, "is how don't you?"

Bane ran his hand over his short-cut waves. Damn near close to falling off of that tight rope he had been balancing on for so long, he hissed, "What did she say?"

"Nothing. I just pay attention—unlike your real nanny, who I couldn't pick out of a lineup because I've never seen her ass." This allowed her to raise finger number four. "And lastly, you know better than anyone how superstitious sports fans are. The minute the Mavericks lose one game after First Down tanks, they're going to see you as bad luck." Dahl was now holding up the fingers of her whole hand.

"These, Bane Carter, are all your fucking problems." She waved at him before she strode out of his office.

With no ammo to lob in her direction, he stayed silent as she slammed his door shut behind her.

* * * *

The staff of First Down had already left for the night. Dahl went over the inventory for the next day. She made a few more tweaks to the menu that had been a big hit.

As soon as the staff got the routine down pat, she would cut back on her hours at the restaurant. Unfortunately, cleaning up First Down and Bane's life soaked up all her free time.

"Dolly, girl, I have the perfect add to the menu," the manager sang on her way through the kitchen doors. Beth's blonde updo, studious glasses and red lipstick fooled most, except Dahl knew better. The woman had no business running a restaurant.

"Dahl… My name is Dahl. Why is that so hard?" she muttered.

"Just trying to be friendly," she cooed. "So I wanted to help with the menu. I have some ideas. Would you like to grab a drink while we hash this out?"

Burned out and ready to spend a week in bed, Dahl felt a twinge of a headache behind her right eye. "No."

"No to the drink or no to—"

"Shit"—she rolled her eyes—"both."

"Cookbooks and television shows do not make you the leading expert on restaurants." Beth's bubbly personality slipped away, revealing the controlling loon who squatted beneath.

"No, but my four years at Le Cordon Bleu and a master's in restaurant management and culinary science makes me the only expert in this room."

Red blotches inched their way up Beth's neck. Before she opened her mouth, someone pushed open the door. "Dahl, you have a visitor," the bartender said.

Sweetly smiling at Beth, Dahl stripped her chef's coat off and laid it across the chair. "Look, Bethy. Do me a favor and stay out of the kitchen. I'm sure the customers love your…teeth." She waved her hand dismissively at the woman and left her to stew. Honestly, Dahl couldn't think of one nice thing to say. For the life of her, she didn't know why her cousin hadn't fired Beth yet.

Dahl stepped into the main dining hall. Sleek and stylish, First Down catered to mid- to high-end customers. Big-screen TVs were mounted on the walls of each private dining area. While great care had been put into the appearance of the place, their initial menu had sucked. No one wanted to pay for overpriced but average nachos.

Stepping farther into the room, she saw the back of Bane's enormous build. Goosebumps tickled her arms. She had no idea where the warm sensation had come from, nor did she want to explore the true source of that emotion.

"You want one?" he asked while he held up his tumbler of Hennessy. Dahl shook her head and slipped behind the bar.

"Do you mind?" She hiked her thumb at the bottles of liquor.

"Help yourself." The bartender closed his register. "I'm officially off the clock." He saluted them goodnight before leaving them alone.

As Bane nursed his drink, Dahl put together the ingredients for a White Russian. Once she'd finished, she leaned against the bar's railing and waited for him to talk.

"Why are you saving these idiots?"

Tired and frustrated, Dahl chuckled. She had no energy to keep up the false narrative that Melanie and Trey weren't complete assholes. "You first." She pointed at him. "And make it good. The clock's ticking."

Bane stared into the mouth of his glass. "Sometimes you get so busy with your own crap you forget that helping certain people ends up hurting them in the long run," he said, finishing his drink. Dahl reached for the expensive brandy in the cabinet and poured him another. "But unlike myself, you, Dahl Hamilton, knew better."

"Knee-jerk reaction," she replied, watering down a more truthful answer.

He raised his right eyebrow, probably in disbelief, but she didn't care. Sticking to her guns, Dahl didn't waver.

"Are you sure that's all it is?" Over the rim of his drink, Bane's hazel-colored eyes held hers before he tipped the glass to his mouth to start round two. Taking in the sight of his full lips, she was shot straight to the past. Dahl remembered how strong and sweet his mouth felt against hers. Shaking the memory away, she tried to focus on the topic at hand.

"Yep." Positive that a spark of the old Bane had appeared for a fleeting second, Dahl took a sip of her drink. It was strong and smooth, so she was already contemplating another round—perhaps she'd finish the whole bottle—anything to keep her mind off the dark copper warrior in front of her.

"How long will it take for you to get this place together?" Bane scanned the empty dining room. Dahl tried to see it from his point of view. It was aesthetically spot on. Melanie had designed it with cream-colored seats that complemented the mahogany tables. She couldn't knock her cousin's style, but she had very little to say about her business sense.

"A new staff has been put into place. They'll be ready to take over soon enough."

"Then what?"

Dahl knew what he was hinting at. If First Down didn't succeed, it wouldn't be her problem. "Hopefully Melanie and Trey will figure it out before I leave."

"Yeah, you hold that thought." He finished off his brandy with a hiss.

"Another?" Dahl asked.

Bane didn't respond. Instead, he stood up and scratched the back of his head. "I didn't know about Ester, and to lose her would—" He shook his head. "The nanny is temporary. We've burned through so many that the agency is reluctant to send me anyone else. I have to stick it out through the contractual terms with her, then we can move on to someone more suitable."

"That makes sense." She snorted.

When he chuckled, the heaviness in the room shifted. "As soon as I get more staff, you're off the hook."

"Is that an apology?"

"Nah." As a slim smile graced his handsome face, Bane rubbed his thumb over his bottom lip. "I figured you were in the business of doling out favors, so what's one more?" He tapped the bar with his finger before he took off. "See you, Dahl."

Chapter Four

For the entire drive home, one sexy chef had stayed heavy on his mind. He'd never thought she would take the bait and cook for his family. Betting on her ego, he'd believed she wouldn't allow herself to be anyone's personal chef. Nevertheless, his strategy to appear affable had failed. If he wanted her gone, he would need a different approach. Unfortunately, it had become all too clear that he needed her around.

As Bane tried to shake off the effects she still had on him, he wrestled with the front door and stepped into his foyer. The television blared. Less than a year ago, Friday nights hadn't resembled a 1980s movie filled of teenage hormones and neglect.

Back then, Fridays had been the gatekeeper of the coveted weekend. However, four kids and one dysfunctional team screwed up any plans for him to chill.

"Uncle Bane!" Cady, who stood on the stair's mid-level landing, quickly climbed onto the wood railing. "Catch me."

"No, no, no."

The little girl did a graceful leap over the bannister. Panic flooded his system before he stepped to the right and caught her. "Omph." He took a hit to the chest.

She laughed hysterically.

"Don't do that again," Bane admonished her. "If I had missed you—"

"But you didn't... You're a supa hero. That's what Daddy always said."

He fought against the smile that erased his serious expression. Most days he could keep the grief at bay, but he missed his baby brother. Bane walked down the hall. Five teenagers filled the room with their loud personalities, phones and popcorn.

"Ladies."

"Hi, Mr. Carter," everyone unrelated to him chimed back in unison.

"Not that I don't enjoy seeing your shiny faces, but it's time to let your parents get tired of you."

"Uncle Bane!" Alana screamed in protest.

"It's cool," the smallest but bossiest of the pack said. "We have to get going."

They gathered their belongings from the floor, leaving a tornado of teenage mess behind.

"Sorry about that. He's so-o embarrassing." Alana flicked her curly black hair over her shoulder and walked her friends to the door.

"No prob. Don't forget about the lock-in," the girl in charge told her.

Too pretty and arrogant for her own good, Alana had made friends fast, but he doubted they were the type to stick around long.

"Uncle Bane!" the fifteen-year-old called after him with a syrupy sweet tone as he headed up the stairs with Cady.

"If you don't want the answer to be no, I suggest you don't ask me right now."

"That's not fair," she whined.

"Go pick up your friends' crap," he told her. An explosive teenage growl accompanied by a good couple of stomps across his tiled floor came next. Bane tried his level best to ignore her.

"Mommy called it tempertals," Cady put in, with her usual creative command of language.

"Temperamental." Bane laughed at the cute kiddie way that she'd pronounced the word and switched her into the position of a football.

"That's what I said."

He stopped at the thirteen-year-old boy's bedroom door. The kid didn't have much interest in sports, so Bane barely had anything in common with Jarin. As he talked on his headset to someone in some far-off land, he beat the pads to his video game controller to death.

"How long have you been on that thing?" Bane asked him.

"One second, Unc."

"In about two I'm going to rip that thing out of the wall. Get off."

"Ah-h, crap." Jarin threw his hands up. "No, I got to go. Yeah, he's making me." He spoke into his headphones, ignoring Bane for the most part.

Busy with all things football, Bane honestly hadn't spent that much time with his brother's family. These kids were practically strangers.

"Daddy used to say the same thing," Cady shared.

Bane reached down and patted the munchkin's head, not at all surprised. He and his brother had often received that same treatment growing up. Walking on down the hallway, he came to the nursery. His brother and wife had died a few months after the birth of their fourth child.

"Hey, beautiful." His house manager for the last fifteen years, Ester, had survived one of his marriages and three franchise trades. However, he felt the acquisition of four kids would send her into an early retirement. The old woman sat in the middle of the nursery, rocking the baby to sleep with her eyes closed. Reaching to shut the door, Ester's stern voice stopped him.

"That woman you hired left early again."

"You're shi-ii—" He glanced down to Cady's smiling face. One slip-up would cost him five dollars. Since Dahl had arrived, the rate had gone up. If he didn't get his act together, he would be in the poor house by fall. *Stupid curse jar.* "You're kidding me, right?"

"No, sir. You're going to have to do something about her. And remember that tonight there's no nurse." He opened his mouth, to plead his case for her to stay, but she held up her hand to stop him. "Don't bother."

Normally thin, her small frame now held very little fat. He took in the slender woman who suddenly appeared gaunt. Heaviness settled into his chest. Dahl had him dead to rights. He had been too caught up in his own life and missed all the signs. "Is everything okay?"

"Fine. Why do you ask?"

"No reason." He knew she would never confess. "Maybe you should move into the house. It would make it easier."

"For who, you? Because there aren't enough ways for me to say no to that." She got up slowly and put the baby in the crib. "And don't bother offering me a driver, because it's not going to happen."

"Ester—" he began.

"Now, dear, I told you that I don't plan on sticking around very much longer. I'm old, and Alabama or Tennessee are nice, warm places." She patted the baby on the back before she made her way to the door.

"How about you stick around until Cady graduates from college?" he suggested. "I'll throw in a few extra coins."

"Sorry, dear, but no dice." Ester grabbed her coat off the rack and handed him the baby monitor. "You should start looking for another nanny, ASAP."

"Got it."

"Oh, and that new cook is a treat. Try not to run her off with your personality."

"Sorry… The outlook is cloudy on that front," he admitted. Under no circumstances did he want Dahl to stick around.

As Ester passed by, she patted him on the arm. Once she cleared out for the night, he would be on his own until morning.

"Now what?" the preschooler asked. Nearly forgetting about the kid in the crook of his arm, he sighed.

"Getting you ready for bed, that's what."

"No-o, just a little longer." She pretended to doggy paddle in his arms.

It was easier to give in than to negotiate with a four-year-old, so he nodded. "Okay." Bane chuckled. The kid cracked him up. "But don't get used to it."

"Yay!" she cheered.

* * * *

Three weeks later

The weather shot from a chilly fifty degrees straight to the eighties. Players from the Mavericks strolled into and around Bane's house for a quick game of touch football. It had taken a couple of weeks for Dahl to figure it out, but she had a routine down. Sundays she dedicated to food prep, including instructions on how to reheat each dish. The rest of her time would either be spent at the restaurant or creating recipes for her cookbook.

"It just seems a little unprofessional is all," the nanny said.

Dahl slid the chicken into the freezer before she turned her attention toward Chelle, who was no older than twenty-five. Dahl had finally gotten the honor of meeting her the previous week.

The phantom nanny toyed with the Granny Smith apples on the counter, one of which Dahl plucked out of her hand.

"Hey!" she pouted. "Mr. Carter requested you wear an apron or smock."

"That's strange. He didn't say anything to me." Not that Dahl had crossed paths with Bane since their little talk. Regardless, she decided to call the nanny's bluff.

"Well, he wanted me to tell you, so that's what I'm doing." She sniffed.

"Okay, I'll wait until he says it to my face." Dahl knew she came off more than a little intimidating. Standing at a good five feet ten inches with huge breasts and ass, she would never be confused for a Tinkerbell. She didn't have the time or the inclination to shrink away from her size, so she kept her body toned and her approach bold as fuck. However, not everyone enjoyed that outcome.

After she sliced the apples, she moved on to the egg mixture for the pie.

"Mr. Carter doesn't like to be challenged. If I were you, I would listen." Chelle threw her long hair over her shoulder and stuck her petite little nose in the air.

"If I have to wear a chef's coat, then what about you?"

"Huh?" Chelle responded in a clueless, immature manner.

"I'm not an expert, but don't nannies generally wear thick coats, with an umbrella and a hat?"

"Wha-a-a?"

"Oh no, that's Mary Poppins. My bad."

The girl's brows pinched together in confusion. "I don't know who that is."

"Of course you don't," Dahl announced sadly, working hard not to burst into laughter. "In other words, if a rule is instituted for me to wear a uniform, then the same mandate would have to be placed on the whole staff. Judging by that cute little blouse you're wearing, I'm sure a nanny's uniform would ruin the whole look."

"What? That's not true," Chelle huffed. "I'm going to talk to Mr. Carter about this."

"You should do that." Dahl threw the apples into the mixture she'd prepared earlier. After coating the fruit pieces with flour and spices, she shook them into the pie crust. "But first you should—I don't know—maybe go check on the kids."

"What are you implying?"

Worse than Alana by a mile. Dahl wondered how bad the other applicants for the nanny job had been in comparison. Hopefully Bane's taste hadn't taken a pathetic turn toward pure laziness dressed in a flowy top and coochie-cutter shorts.

"It sounds like she's calling you a slacker." Ester stepped into the room with her sweater and purse draped over her arm. "Which would be one hundred percent accurate. Now go find something to do and leave Dahl alone. I don't want her ruining my pie."

After Chelle stormed off, Ester turned to Dahl. "I had a feeling she would be sniffing around you. That girl's been hitting on Bane for weeks. He'd do himself a huge favor by getting rid of her, pronto. How's my pie coming?" She rubbed her hands together.

"It should be all set for your bake-off tomorrow."

Pure elation slid across Ester's face. "My church won't know what hit them."

"Full disclosure…" Dahl chastised the woman for cheating. "You should be ashamed of yourself."

"Well, I'm not. That derelict Sister Rose wins every year and that woman can't boil water. She has a ringer, plain and simple. There's no reason why I shouldn't either."

One of the football players opened the patio door, interrupting their lighthearted banter. "Excuse me, ladies, but Bane isn't here yet and we need someone to pick the teams," the rookie stated.

"That's my cue," Ester said, while jerking her thumb in Dahl's direction. "This one here will help you."

"What are we doing, a scrimmage?" Dahl crisscrossed the top dough over the apples. The touch football game at the coach's house was tradition. It dated all the way back to Bane's college days.

"Yeah, do you mind?"

"Let me get this pie into the oven first." Pure joy filled her soul. Dahl knew better than anyone that Bane would hate that she'd played along.

Chapter Five

At the end of every season, directly before training camp, Bane invited members from the Mavericks' current roster over for a game of touch football. It helped him assess what areas they needed to improve during camp. Unfortunately, one of his defensive linemen had gotten hurt in an ATV accident.

"Bossman," the assistant coach greeted him in front of the driveway. Luxury cars lined his street and blocked his driveway. "How's the big guy doing?"

Bane had just come from the hospital. "He needs more testing and is probably out for the fall season, if not for his career." He'd warned these boneheads about their off-season activities, but no one ever took him seriously until it was too late.

"Sheesh, that's tough. But on a lighter note, the first half of our game is almost over and that chef of yours has got one hell of a—"

"What?"

"Yeah, the coach versus your chef, who looks awfully familiar, by the way."

Pinching the bridge of his nose, Bane sighed. "Tell me she's not winning?"

"Laying him flat." The assistant laughed. "And the coach is fuming."

Bane picked up his pace and shot around the side of the house. He hit the backyard in record time to witness Dahl's team scoring another touchdown. He nodded at a couple of the players on the sidelines but kept his sight on his gorgeous goal. Bane headed straight for Dahl Hamilton. Unfortunately, it wasn't warm fuzzies that coursed through his veins. Instead, panicked desperation had settled into his chest and snuggled there.

"What are you doing?" he muttered. *Besides standing here looking incredibly hot*, he finished in his head. Big, glossy curls framed her face, flowing over her shoulders, while her awesome breasts stretched the fabric of her black tank top.

"Duh, touch football game." She rolled her eyes and gestured toward his players.

"No-o, you're winning," Bane growled through clenched teeth, while he kept a phony smile in place. "It undermines the coach."

"The arrogant ass should have picked a better team," she told him.

Dahl knew as well as he did how to play the game. It was her father who had taught him the business of football. Right now, he honestly didn't need this crap, but it was too late now. He chose to just watch the rest of the carnage. *Please, let this be over soon.*

As Bane stood on the sideline joking with his players, Dahl's team scored the game-winning touchdown. She tried not to gloat but did a little dance in spite of herself.

"Beginner's luck," the Mavericks' coach said with a grimace, which stretched his rough skin even tighter.

"I'm not even sure who does what," Dahl teased, ignoring Bane, who stood behind the coach and mouthed, 'What the fuck?' She bit her bottom lip and shook the coach's hand.

"Rematch?" he demanded through gritted teeth.

"Anytime."

"Whenever your boss here can spare you." The coach zinged her with a petty dig. Obviously, he didn't have the foggiest idea about her football background. His arrogance had forced him to pick the team he thought would beat her. If they didn't make it to the playoffs, the coach had nobody to blame but himself.

"Did you want to stick around for ribs? We've got a caterer coming." Bane patted the coach on his back.

"No, I'm going to the hospital to check on Jimmy." The vein on the side of his head continued to pulsate.

Sore freaking loser. He nodded goodbye and left with a couple of the players, while the rest of the team filed into the house.

"Just this once you could have lost," Bane grumbled, his warm breath sending shivers down her spine, a teenager's reaction to an adult-ass man. They trailed behind the group at a good distance.

"Now what would be the fun in that?"

Giants gathered in the kitchen and on the patio. The group of huge men shrank the size of his substantial mansion by their mere presence. Dahl had already spent more time than she'd planned at Bane's. She still needed to work on recipes for her book. With no intention of staying any longer, she slipped away from the group and stepped into the coatroom.

In a couple of months, the restaurant could run without her. Dahl needed to get started on her next project. She had given up too much of her time to clean up everyone else's mess.

"This pie is banging!" one of the players hollered.

It took a split second for his words to seep into the whirling thoughts inside her head. "Oh shit!" Dropping her purse, she ran out of the room.

"No, no, not the damn pie." She flew into the kitchen, pointing at the maniac who had shoveled nearly an entire slice into his mouth.

"Did you make this, coach lady? Because this is banging." Nothing but crumbs decorated the tin pan that had held Ester's perfectly crafted dessert. "That tiny chick said we could eat it."

"Kid or adult?" she asked, pretty sure she knew the answer.

"Adult, I think. Yeah, tall." He held his hand a little bit higher than Alana's height.

"Chelle," she hissed.

"Sorry." He swallowed the rest of the pie and belched. "But, damn, that was good."

As lingering thoughts of nanny violence swam in Dahl's head, she counted the apples to see if she could throw together another pie.

"Ah-h, has your pie gone bye-bye?" Bane took a messy bite of a Granny Smith close to her ear.

She snatched the empty pie tin off the counter with a vicious growl.

* * * *

48

The players piled out of the house not too long after they had eaten almost everything she'd made that afternoon. Apparently, Ester's pie hadn't been the only treat the shitty babysitter had offered up both to spite her and to pay tribute to the football gods.

While she sliced the apples, Dahl preheated the oven.

"Need help?" Bane asked.

Without waiting for her to answer, he grabbed the rolling pin and worked the dough.

"I heard you won the coin toss but coach had better players on his team. What made you pick yours?"

"Considering that my team won, I disagree." Annoyed that she had to put another week's worth of meals together for the family, she didn't feel much like chit-chat. Dahl shrugged and tossed the apple slices into a bowl.

"Stats... You know what I mean," he muttered.

When she'd met Bane during her first year in college, they had been inseparable. After a few months of dating, she'd introduced him to her father. Hall of Famer Richard Hamilton, AKA Fast Ricky, had become ridiculously wealthy after football by investing in real estate development. Unfortunately, he'd ended up with Parkinson's. Dahl had always had her suspicions that the wear and tear from the game had caused his illness.

"The coach may have had a better team, but he's not exactly a chess player," Dahl pointed out.

"Nope. He believes in strength over good sense."

"His team didn't work together. There's someone throwing them off," she admitted.

Bane nodded his head in agreement. "Why didn't you pick Shawn Mathers?"

As Dahl stirred the sugar mixture into the boiling pot, he laid the crust in the tin and smushed down the dough. "I didn't have a choice. He was coach's numero uno," she replied.

"He's the best player," he told her.

Dahl glanced over her shoulder at Bane. He thumbed the edges of the crust in precisely the way his grandmother had instructed her years ago. They had a long history together. Unfortunately, big egos and white noise had gotten in the way of everything. The news of her father's illness had come on the occasion of Bane's second concussion. Dahl had lost her shit and issued him an ultimatum—the death blow to their already-by-then-shaky union. Nevertheless, she could tell he wanted to pick her brain, but she didn't know why.

"The coach certainly seems to think he is."

Bane threw her a crooked, sexy smile that warmed her insides. Before she thawed out totally toward him, she took the apples and dumped them into the pot.

"We added a training camp to the schedule in a couple of weeks," he said.

The aroma of the sweet apples wafted throughout the kitchen. "That's generally how it goes." Dahl flipped off the burner.

"It's more like a retreat—and we don't have a cook."

"Come on, Bane." She threw the dish towel over her shoulder with a hiss and brought the pot over to the chef's island. "Cooking for the entire Carter squad isn't blackmail enough?"

"We're good after this." He stared at her with hooded eyes. "I promise."

Big and powerful, he commanded attention, even with the slight upward tilt of his lips. The sexy request almost fooled her into believing him. A tug in her gut whispered for her to not only flirt back but to conquer Bane Carter.

"What did I miss? Is there a fabulous live-in cooking nanny ready to swoop in?" She pointed at him. "Oh shit, is she Jamaican? I know you have a thing for them." If she remembered correctly, ex-wife number two had made a public spectacle with their divorce. The woman was also something exotic, but she couldn't quite remember what.

He shook his head with a chuckle. "No, I'm sure it's time for you to get back to your life."

"Which means what? You proved your point." Waiting for the mix to cool, Dahl swirled the filling in the pot before she put it in the mason jars. Since she had to come back tomorrow anyway, she decided to let the mix set in the refrigerator.

"Nope. Shit's hard enough around these parts without you pointing a big neon sign at all my shortcomings."

"Just trying to help." Pleased that his plan to screw her over hadn't worked, she threw him a cheeky wink. "But, seriously, if I do this, no backsies."

"Deal." He held his hand across the chef's island to her. Dahl accepted his peace treaty. Competitive to a fault, Bane hated to lose, but he would have to concede defeat, since she had definitely whooped him in their little game of petty exes.

Chapter Six

As a wicked storm raged outside, the spring season flew in with a roar. They were inching closer to summer vacation, and the kids had off for another freaking teachers' conference. Dahl balanced the food tray on her arm and worked her way upstairs.

Dahl was fresh off the phone with her agent. Trish had offered her two different food competitions to judge. Dahl had told her she would think about it. In reality, she hoped her producer, Jeff, would come up with a better concept for a television project.

"Here you go, sweet pea." The little girl barely glanced away from *Timmy Time*, a cartoon on the television. Dahl set the mug of homemade cocoa on her dresser.

"Marshmallows?"

"Of course," she answered, slightly offended at the adult child's attitude.

"Thank you, Dolly."

"No problem, toots." She went down the hall to Alana's room and pushed the door open. "Cocoa."

"Dahl, I have an idea for a makeup tutorial. Will you help me?" Alana sat in front of her vanity, playing with her eyelash curler.

"Sure. Write me a proposal on how your tutorial will be different than the millions already out there and include your main goal. If I think it's good enough, I'll hold the phone."

"Really? I can just ask Cady."

"True, but between the back and forth, bad angles and giggling, it will look like shit." She handed the girl the copper mug full of chocolate-kissed dreams.

"Fine," she whined with an amazing amount of teenage pissiness.

"You've got an hour to get it done."

Dahl left Bane's oldest niece's Barbie dream bedroom, heading to his oldest nephew's dark cave. Lightly tapping on the door, she pushed it open.

"What took you so long?" Jarin handed her a remote control and she passed him a mug.

"Sorry... I had to make my way past the cops and the gangbangers."

"Nice try. We're playing Fortnite. No more Grand Theft Auto for you."

She pulled out his bean bag and popped a squat. "Spoilsport." After Jarin had binged all the food, Dahl had made a deal to get him out of his room. She would play a game once a week and cook a dish of his choosing if he sat down for daily dinner with the family. So far, the compromise was working out pretty well and she had managed to bone up on her video game skills in the process.

"I want to enter a competition, but it costs money."

Dahl shot at a demon baseball player. "How are you going to get it?"

"I'm going to ask Uncle Bane."

"Really? Think that will work out in your favor?"

"Nope," Jarin said before he saved her character from a zombie thing he beat to death with a stop sign.

"How about applying for the water boy position with the Mavericks?" she told him.

"They don't get paid."

"No, but you can do little odds and ends around the stadium that will get you money."

"Maybe?" He didn't sound convinced.

"Trust me. Once he sees you're willing to sweat, he'll pay you." Distracted by all the colors, she got taken out fairly quick by a blue dude with an orbed head. "Shit, I suck at this," Dahl admitted. She hated to lose almost worse than Bane.

"Yeah, that's why I picked it."

* * * *

The lights flickered from the rumble of thunder that shook the house. Bane glanced out of his office window at the dark clouds. He wasn't a fan of storms. As he turned his attention back to the computer screen, he tried to ignore the stabbing pain behind his eye that was distracting him from his work.

"Cocoa?" With a mug in hand, Dahl walked into his office.

Bane dropped his head back at the sexy intruder and swallowed his groan. He wanted to tell her no. However, out of all the things he could be accused of, being a fool wasn't one of them. Accepting the cup from the world-renowned chef, he grunted out his thanks.

"Somebody is in a good mood. Is it the storm?" Dahl asked, and shifted a football paperweight on his desk. He breathed in her soft scent of vanilla mixed with some sort of exotic spice and cursed himself. He'd never thought she would agree to this crazy scheme. He'd simply wanted to call her bluff.

After so many years apart, Bane had misinterpreted that initial gut punch of emotion he'd felt once he'd laid eyes on her. Hate may have been a strong emotion, but love was even stronger.

"I'm the general manager of a football team and over forty… I think I'm good."

"Really? Because if I remember correctly —"

"Thanks for the cocoa," he cut her off. Bane took a swig of her smooth chocolate and tried not to groan. *Damn!*

"Ah, you must think I'm one of your employees." She snorted before perching her hip on the edge of his desk closest to him. "Sorry, sweetie. I'm not that easy to get rid of."

No shit. He couldn't get her out of his head. What made him think he could get her out of his office?

As the inside of his skull squeezed his brain, he pinched the bridge of his nose.

"Uncle Bane?"

"Uh-huh?" He opened his eyes. Jarin hovered near the door.

"Never mind. I-I-I can come back later…"

Bane couldn't remember the last time he'd seen the kid outside of his room, and he was curious to see what the boy wanted. "What's up?"

He nervously shifted his weight from one foot to the other. "Um, can I be a water boy for this upcoming season?"

"Oh." Positive Dahl had had something to do with this, he cut his eyes in her direction but said to Jarin, "Can you even catch a — ?"

Before he could finish, Dahl snatched his signed MLB foul ball from the White Sox 2009 no-hitter game and threw it at his nephew.

"Shi-i-i," he hissed, thankful that the kid snagged it out of the air. Bane damn near had a heart attack. He held up his hand for Jarin to toss it back. "Sure." He caught his precious treasure and set it on his desk, far out of Dahl's reach.

"Really?" Jarin's face lit up. No good could come from the boy sniffing out his soft spot.

"Just because you're my nephew doesn't mean you get to slide."

"Got it. Cool!" Jarin ran off.

Feeling more than a little suckered, he took a deep breath and returned his attention to his iMac Pro.

"Ready for the retreat?" Bane asked. His immature plan to embarrass his gorgeous ex no longer held that same warm, fuzzy appeal it once had. Unable to make out the words on the monitor, he resisted the urge to rub his temples.

"Got a headache?" While she dug into her jeans pocket, Dahl side-stepped his question.

"If its name is Dahl Hamilton, I sure do."

"Now, now, be nice or you don't get these." She opened her hand to reveal a small bottle of ibuprofen. The one person who knew why he hated storms stood right in front of him offering help.

Bane didn't think he could make it much longer with Dahl Baby Hamilton in touching distance. He needed to put some space between them — and fast.

Chapter Seven

Dahl mixed the ingredients for the special for the day, crab salad. First Down's regular patrons had preferences. Many of them booked the upper floor for parties or work events once a month, which meant the extra effort she had put in to appease them was truly paying off.

As she finished her mix, Dahl's cell phone buzzed in her pants.

"Money jar," the morning crew yelled in unison.

"Technically I'm not supposed to be here, so it doesn't count." As Dahl put the bowl down, she dug into her pocket and answered her phone.

"Hey, it's me," Bane said, sounding tense.

She headed out of the back door. The white noise from the kitchen made it too hard to hear. "What's up?"

"Uh, Ester is doing something with her church group and I can't find Chelle."

"Shocker." After waving to her bread vendor, who was pulling away from the alley, Dahl stepped closer to the river ledge. The city was beautiful, even serene, depending the time of day. These were the moments Dahl loved. She loosened the rubber band from her hair and shook out her curls while she waited for Bane to get to the point.

"This is a hard ask, but could you go down to the school and pick up Alana?" he said in a rush. "Apparently some girls took her stuff out of her locker and she got her period, which—"

"Got the idea. I'll shoot over there."

Bane let out a deep sigh. "You're a life saver."

"Sure." She hung up without offering any pesky salutations.

"Was that Bane?" Melanie asked.

Dahl turned toward her cousin. "Why?"

"No reason." She puckered her lips as if she'd sucked several lemons.

The staff would need a run-down for the day. Brushing past Melanie on her way back into the kitchen, Dahl tried not to read too much into her funky tone.

"Not that I'm trying to get into your business, but I don't think you should get your hopes up where he's concerned."

Surprised by her audacity, Dahl faced her cousin to make sure she didn't take her the wrong way. Melanie didn't have a genuine bone in her body, and after all these years apart from each other, Dahl didn't believe she had suddenly grown one.

"What makes you say that?"

"This is cousin to cousin." Twisting her face into some sort of emoji sad expression, Melanie attempted to frown. Since the look came off between smelling something bad and confusion, Dahl wasn't sold.

"Oh, is it the free advice time of the day?" Dahl asked, surprised at the pair of balls on her cousin.

"Not that I have concrete proof or anything... I just have a bad feeling that Bane is using you." Melanie dabbed at the corner of her eye and blinked her fake lashes rapidly.

"Yeah..." Dahl turned away. "Are you mad it might interfere with *you* using me?"

Before her cousin made another comment that flipped their innocent conversation into an all-out brawl, Dahl left her in the alley.

* * * *

High schools across the USA were all the same—a pinch of team spirit intertwined with a dash of despair and, sometimes, a sprinkle of joy. Since classes were in session, Dahl's heels echoed down the empty corridors. It had taken her a good forty-five minutes before she'd made it to the school, but she'd needed to pick up provisions.

While she reminisced about her days in school and how much she'd hated every single thing that they had entailed, Dahl pushed open the door to the girls' locker room. The smell of chlorine smacked her in the face. She shook off the shivers from the ghosts of freshman year past.

"Alana?" she whispered. Tiptoeing into the room, she swiveled her head back and forth to peer down the rows of lockers. "Hey?"

Around the third row, she finally stumbled upon the teen. Wearing nothing but a towel, she sat red-faced on the bench.

"Did you bring my Juicy sweats?" she asked. The girl didn't look up from the funky tiled floor.

"No, I bought you an outfit and new makeup."

"Why?" Alana sniffed.

"Because you're going to get all cute and go back to class."

"But everyone knows." As she shook her head, panic seeped into her big, hazel eyes. "Someone stole my stuff out of my locker, and I bled through my gym shorts—"

"Do you know why they messed with your belongings?"

"No, and none of the girls who I thought were my friends are talking to me. I just want to go home." She sobbed, damp tendrils from the shower falling onto her face.

A wave of sadness choked the room. Dahl fought back the urge to comfort her and give in to her demands.

"For whatever reason, they want you to cry and they want you to run. Trust me when I say this, but the most powerful thing that you can do is pay them with dust. There's something about you that is obviously intimidating to them, and they want to crush it."

"But I didn't do anything." She wiped at the streaming tears that ran down her face.

"Wow, the rules must have changed since I went to school. There's actual cause and effect?"

"Huh? This isn't a 'when they go low, we go high' type of speech, is it?"

"Honey, no," she chuckled. "When they go low, you take it to the streets, but you aren't about that life. I suggest you put on these ridiculously cute clothes and go back to class."

"How will that help me?"

"Because those little assholes won't expect your snap back. Confidence is the worst take-down in high school. Trust me." Alana's lip trembled, but Dahl could tell she'd begun to consider her offer. "At lunch, go sit with a new group of kids. Ask them questions about teachers or electives for next year and don't look bothered."

"That's not a bad idea." Alana shrugged her small shoulders.

"What do you think about me straightening your hair while you get started on your makeup?"

It took a few seconds, but Alana finally granted her a weak nod and a smile.

"Cool," Dahl said. She put her hand out for Alana to take. They had twenty minutes until the next period.

* * * *

Even in the off-season, Bane had work. He'd finalized the team's draft picks that morning with Coop and the coach. They'd acquired a couple of guys he hadn't totally signed off on, but considering he was often odd man out, he'd let it go.

A light tap on his door dragged his attention away from the mound of crap on his desk. "Am I disturbing you?" Dahl poked her head into his office. That fluttery sensation of warmth that shot through his system dissipated the minute he remembered what he'd had her do for him.

"That depends," he replied.

She opened the door wide enough to slip through and shut it behind her. Bane drank in the sight of her effortless beauty. She was sporting a curly top bun with a couple of loose strands, accompanied by her signature leather jacket and jeans.

"If this leads to an ex-wife-style cuss out, I will have to politely decline this visit."

She held up a greasy white bag. "Chill, Carter. I come in peace."

His stomach rumbled at the thought of food. The sweet offering meant she needed to butter him up for something. Going against his better judgment, he held out his hand. The smell of chicken parmigiana filled his nose.

"Jimmy's," he groaned. Bane dug into the sack. He would have to work out extra hard after this greasy mess. "You're not going to have any?"

"No." She took the seat across from his desk. "I have a date with a toddler later. I'm sure she'll want to eat something equally as bad."

Too busy shoving the best tasting fries into his mouth, he nearly forgot to breathe. "So-o good." Unwrapping the sub, he took a bite and damn near swayed from the delicious taste of it.

"Good?" She nodded.

"The best." He grabbed the thin napkin and wiped the marinara sauce from the sides of his lip. "Thanks again for this morning. We were in negotiations for our draft picks, and Ester was at church—"

"Ester wasn't at church. She just tells you 'church' so you don't ask too many questions."

"Seriously?" He sat back in his seat, stunned that the old woman would be so deceitful—and so good at it. "Let me guess. You came here to tell me how I'm dropping the ball in every aspect of my life."

"Uh, no. I came here because you seemed stressed, so I brought you a sammich."

He bit off another chunk from the sub and tried to digest what she'd said. In the world he moved in, people had hidden agendas, they spoke in code or genuinely wanted to do harm to others. Bane had almost forgotten not to view everyone as his opponent.

"Devon's birthday is this week, and a lot of stuff has been bothering me about our relationship," he told her.

"Such as?" Dahl asked.

"He came to see me the night I jacked up my ACL."

"The night you told the coach not to let me into the ambulance." She pointed at him.

"More like the night you grabbed your shit out of the house and left."

Dahl had the nerve to chuckle at his pain.

"That's funny?" he grunted around a mouthful of fries.

"Yes," she said in a matter-of-fact manner, "it is. Now, please continue."

"My brother had stopped by for advice. He'd gotten Isabella pregnant and he was scared. I was too zonked out on pain pills to really give a shit."

"It's fifteen years later. Why are you in your fee-fees about this now?"

Bane wondered why he'd even brought it up. The only explanation he could think of was that Dahl had always been a good listener and the fast food made him weak. "I was trying to figure the exact moment I checked out, and I think it was around that time. These kids are virtual strangers, the closest relative to me is my house manager, who isn't even blood, and I bribed my ex-wife to cook for a whole household. I'm seriously ill-equipped to deal with a teenage girl's period."

"The problem was a little bigger than that."

"No doubt, but I still couldn't have handled it."

"I'd beg to differ," Dahl told him.

"Regardless… I'm usually on top of everything, but lately," he admitted, more to himself than anyone else, "all of this is way over my head."

A small smile played at the corners of Dahl's mouth. "Don't forget that your nanny seriously sucks! I mean, if there was a shitty nanny contest, she would win."

Bane threw his head back and laughed hard. If nothing else, Dahl was always good for a trash pep talk—and he meant *trash*.

Chapter Eight

The sun beamed down on the University of Illinois field. Taking a much-needed break, Dahl caught the tail end of practice. It made no sense to hold a retreat this close to camp. From what she could tell, management wanted to make cuts.

"Bosslady!" one of the rookies shouted to her in the stands. She waved at the newbie. "My grandma loved that creamsicle pound cake you made. It really lifted her spirits."

"Oh, I'm glad. How she's doing?"

"Better. The doctors are adjusting her medication to see if it will help her MS. I just wish I could spend more time with her before the season starts."

"Jones!" the defense coach yelled, "back to work."

"Oh crap. Well, thanks again."

She waved goodbye to the rookie and locked eyes with Bane. *Don't smile, don't wave... Don't smile, don't wave...* she chanted in her head. There was no way she would go out like a dreamy teen mooning over the star football player

"Too bad the kid doesn't realize he's on the chopping block." The frat boy cadence of the voice caused her to cringe. Dahl shifted her gaze away from the piece of rookie eye candy and toward the Mavericks' most popular player—and sleazebag quarterback. He sat down on the bench mere inches away.

Quarterback Shawn Mathers could have his pick of women and usually did. Needless to say, Dahl had to bury the urge to screech like a cat in his presence. If anyone took the time to study the empty depths of his pretty green eyes, they would see the soulless demon that squatted there. She had encountered plenty of such psychopaths in the past. Easily bored, they generally moved on to their next target quickly.

"He's young. He'll work it out," she defended the country boy.

Shawn was freshly showered and out of uniform, beads of water slipping down the side of his head. "Looks like you have a soft spot for the simpletons. Did you learn that from your dad or underneath our illustrious GM?" As he threw her a slick smile, Dahl stood to leave.

"Ah, come on." He grabbed her by the elbow. "I'm just kidding. Take a seat."

She didn't want to appear weak. Sick freaks like him got off on the smell of fear.

"I've got to get dinner ready." She yanked her arm out of his grip. "But, hey, good talk." She forced the smallest smile onto her face and headed back to the cafeteria. Positive he was still watching her, she beat off the urge to break into a sprint.

* * * *

On the field players slammed into the practice dummies. From the sidelines Bane had caught Shawn slipping away. The asshole was always drawn to the shiniest toy, so Bane had no doubt what his quarterback had gone after—Dahl.

"That boy is simply not cutting it," the coach said.

"What boy? I don't think we drafted any children."

"Don't try that shit with me, Winston. I was born and bred in the North. My family doesn't have a single racist bone in our family tree."

Bane chuckled at the absurdity of his statement. "If I'm stuck with Mathers, you can at least keep A.J. through camp. If he doesn't get better, then we'll cut him."

"Shawn may get into trouble from time to time, but he still pulls his weight. What's this really about?" The condescending shithead tapped him on the shoulder with his clipboard. "Are you jealous of his stats?" The coach laughed. Bane knew he meant for him to take that personally.

"Unlike yourself, I know what it's like to actually play in the league." He poked at the coach's less-than-stellar college career. "One guy won't drag a NCAA team down, but the at pros are different." He shook his head. "The stupid shit Shawn pulls can cost us the whole season. He's good, but not that good."

"He's my guy," the coach growled, "and I have the full weight of Coop behind me on this."

Bane knew he was the odd man out. "Hm-m, he's not your *boy*?" He threw the coach's own words back at the arrogant ass. "Vouch for him all you want. His next fuck up is on you." Stepping away from the foolish man, Bane glanced back at the stands.

* * * *

Never predictable, spring weather in the Midwest was always cold, then ended toward mildly less cold. Since the team was working out in an unexpected eighty-degree heat, Dahl had planned out a hearty, royal feast to send them off on their vacation.

"A competition show will keep your profile up while you're off saving the world," her agent said.

As Trish tried to pitch her on several fruitless endeavors, she shook the seasoning mix over the shish kabobs. Dahl planned to cook the large sticks on the grill out back. The girlfriends and wives were expected to join the players for their luau.

"Ha-ha. I'm just saving my cousin's restaurant. Sarcasm not required."

"My awesome wit is the only thing that holds your attention. It will be the fastest and easiest money you've ever earned. Think about it," Trish said before she hung up.

"Love you, too, sweetie," Dahl replied in a mocking tone.

"Terms of endearment? I thought we would at least get to the second date before that." Shawn stepped into the kitchen with a lopsided smirk.

Her strong distaste for the player was what probably led her to envision the Batman villain Two-Face every time she laid eyes on him.

"A second date? Now that seems lofty." Dahl palmed the knife from her prep station. Considering the team had another hour of practice, he didn't have a good reason to follow her to the cafeteria.

"Believe me... You'll want to stay in my bed after the first one."

Dahl nodded at the food. "You know how a hungry team gets, so if you don't mind..." The hard thud of her heart racing inside of her chest set her teeth on edge. Dahl swallowed down her fear.

"Since you brought up hunger... I'm in need of a chef." Shawn slunk closer to her. The football field was three buildings away. No one would hear her scream. Tall and built, the quarterback would catch Dahl before she made it out of the room. Shawn plucked a peach out of the fruit bowl she had planned to use to decorate the table.

"Let me finish up here and I'll get you a list of chefs—"

"Nah, I don't want any-old-body." He stepped closer, boxing her into the prep station. "I want what the GM has, and what's good enough for him."

Dahl kept the knife clutched tightly underneath the table. She didn't want to stab him, but the rumors that circled the player forced her to be willing to err on the side of caution.

"Practice is almost over." Shawn took a sloppy bite out of the peach and smacked obnoxiously close to her face. His hot breath heated her ear. "We can leave or stick around. It's up to you." the QB's smug grin slipped into a sneer.

"Mathers, Coach is looking for you," Bane said.

Turning his head, Shawn spat out the peach pit he'd been sucking on. "Needed something to hold me over."

"Now that you've gotten it, get lost," Bane said.

Regardless of the strong energy that choked the room, Dahl released a breath.

As Shawn slowly backed out of the kitchen, he kept his eyes on her. "Catch you later, Dahl." He turned around and left them alone.

Larger than life, Bane gently bumped her from behind. The closeness calmed the waves of anxiety that had set fire to her skin at the sight of the quarterback.

"You okay?" The softened timbre of his voice immediately settled her nerves.

Far from it, Dahl thought, but she nodded. She needed to finish dinner and shake off the itchy feeling.

"Why don't you go home? We can wrap up this retreat with takeout." He stood ridiculously close to her. She found the heat from his body comforting.

"No" —she cleared her throat— "I'm good."

"Are you cooking at the restaurant's charity event?" He probably wanted to change the subject. She knew better than to turn around. The slightest indication of sympathy would leave her in a puddle of shaky nerves and tears.

"Uh, yeah." Dahl reached with her free hand for the fruit bowl. "I'll be overseeing the kitchen and menu."

"Great. I strong-armed our cousins into holding it at First Down. It's for my foundation, True Warriors. One last thing before you go back to your life, I guess." The warmth of his calloused hand slipped down her arm. "Are you sure you're okay?"

Licking her lips, she tried to resist his touch. "Yep," she said, throwing him a weak smile.

Bane covered her hand with his. "Cool. I mean, you usually have everything under control." He grabbed the handle of the knife out of her hand and plunged it into the watermelon. "Holler if you need anything."

Without engaging in some sort of touchy-feely conversation, he placed the coaching team's walkie talkie on the table next to her. Before she could turn around to face him, Bane had walked out of the kitchen.

Chapter Nine

Low candlelight created an intimate ambiance throughout First Down. The restaurant was filled to the brim with wealthy donors. Bane mingled among Chicago's elite. His charity paid tuition and fees for inner-city children to attended after-school programs. Passionate about his project, he worked the room, determined to get the tightwads to loosen the grips on their wallets. Bane chatted up a widow of one of the Mavericks' most ardent fans, hoping she would allow some of those millions to flow toward his cause.

"My Harold loved everything about the Mavericks, even those ridiculous beer hats. He stopped wearing them years ago but kept collecting them for his man cave, if you can believe that." Without much to offer her besides the boilerplate sympathy platitudes, Bane simply nodded.

"Hey, I need to talk to you for a minute." Andre Burnett, his relief running back, tapped him on the shoulder.

"Excuse me, Gloria," he told his potential donor and followed the player to the bar. "What's going on?"

"This second fiddle act to your busted vets isn't doing me any favors. My contract is up next year, and no one worth a shit is going to sign me unless I get my stats up."

"What do you want from me?" Apparently one night without this shit was too much to ask. Bane ordered a shot of Patrón.

"The coach won't play me, and you know I'm better than Greg's sorry ass. Not to mention that Shawn's grimy antics are bound blow up in management's faces."

Bane glanced across the room. The quarterback was holding court over a group of fans, his cousin Trey among them. The urge to bust his face in hadn't left him since he'd found him sniffing around Dahl.

"Look… I'm a team player when there's an actual team," Andre said. "There's no way that fool should still be here."

"If I put in a good word for you, it will only make it worse." Bane tossed the rest of his drink down his throat and ordered another.

"They told me this would be a waste of my time," Andre grumbled.

Bane caught a glimmer of Dahl through the slit of the swinging door. She looked amazing. The last time he'd seen her, she'd had one hell of a grip on a knife, which brought him back to the conversation at hand…Shawn Mathers. Rumors about his aggressive tendencies had floated around the locker room. Bane had never been able to get concrete evidence to back up the stories. A suspicious inkling told him that the Mavericks' owner and coach had paid off more than their fair share of women. Without a police report, he couldn't do anything about the sycophant .

"Ladies and gentlemen, welcome to the first fundraiser of True Warrior Boys Club," Melanie informed the room. A skinny, sharp version of Dahl stood in front of the enormous fireplace. "We have several silent auctions tonight, but first we need to thank my cousin and famous chef, Dahl Hamilton, for our fantastic food this evening." The audience clapped for the beauty, but he saw no sign of her.

"Look… You're a good player. I'll do what I can. If it's with the Mavericks or another team, I'll figure something out."

Andre nodded his head. "Cool. Look… We get it. You're the first black GM in the league, so I thought I'd warn you—"

The over-enthusiastic blonde who ran the restaurant tried to tug Dahl out of the kitchen.

"A couple of us are planning to kneel at the start of the season."

"Sounds about right," Bane responded to the icing on the cake before he signaled for one more drink. His goal to get slightly buzzed appeared to be within arm's reach.

"Just thought you should know, so you can work on whatever bullshit statement they're going to make you say at the press conference."

The blonde tried to drag Dahl toward her cousin—a fruitless effort, considering the huge size difference. While they struggled, the woman managed to work Dahl's chef coat off, revealing a skin-tight number that hugged her every curve. Taking her spot next to Melanie, Dahl offered a shy wave to the crowd.

"We auctioned off a date with the chef, to her surprise and my great pleasure." Melanie held her hand to the side of her mouth. "She's not getting any younger," she said to lukewarm laughter.

As Bane checked the attendants' reactions, he inadvertently made eye contact with Shawn. The quarterback provided him a salute with his drink.

"We're doing a date with the chef first because, trust me, she'll ghost us and him in a matter of seconds." Melanie smiled a little too brightly. "I can't name the highest bidder since they requested anonymity, but I can tell you they donated a whopping twenty-five thousand dollars to the True Warriors Boys Club." This time, the applause thundered. "Now on to the next auction."

* * * *

Bane stood at the restaurant door and personally shook hands with everyone who had attended his fundraiser. They'd raised over eight hundred and fifty thousand dollars for the True Warriors Boys Club. Nothing, not even Shawn Mathers, could dampen his mood. When he was pretty sure everyone had left, he decided to call it a night. Bane headed for the coat check.

"I thought you left already," he said to Dahl, who was waiting in front of the closet.

"I've been too busy looking for my anonymous date so I can pay him back."

"Don't be a chauvinist, Dahl. It could have been a woman." Bane grabbed Dahl's coat from the attendant and handed over his ticket. "You look great, by the way."

As he held her coat open, Dahl turned around. "Not like one of your Barbies, but great for someone who cuts onions for living," she muttered.

One at a time, she put each arm into her mid-length velvet number. "Who said you weren't a Barbie?"

"I don't fit into that box," she admitted, before straightening her collar and turning around to face him.

Without a thought, he reached over to move a wayward curl out of her face. Every moment in her presence chipped away at his resolve. His mind commanded his legs to move but they didn't. "There's no box that could ever hold you."

"Are you curvy-girl-shaming me?"

Bane laughed. He honestly couldn't tell if she was serious or not. When they had been in college, hot couldn't describe her. Damn near twenty years later, Dahl had turned into something far beyond sexy.

Another minute in her presence and he would take her against the wall. Conquering enough problems for a lifetime, let alone a day, he refused to allow this molehill to become a mountain, so he grabbed his coat from the attendant. "Good night, Dahl."

* * * *

Dahl tried but failed to get out of her anonymous date. Three days had already passed and she still didn't know who had won the bid. Anxious to get it over with, she arranged a meeting spot through the manager of First Down.

Thankfully, the temperature that night was fairly mild. She waited not too far from Wicker Park to start the clock on this creep-tastic experience. She stood near Wrigley Field, home of the Cubs, and tried to estimate the amount of time that would be considered appropriate before she bailed. *Fifteen minutes? Ten minutes? Hell, even five.* Technically, her escort for the evening had three minutes until their official meet time. Considering the date was for charity, how bad would it look if she ran like a mad woman?

"Is this your typical date attire?"

Dahl turned at the sound of Bane's deep baritone voice. She had never been happier to see him in her whole life. Fighting back the urge to tackle him and kiss him silly, she shoved a handful of her curls out of her face and took in the sexy sight of her ex-husband.

The big man appeared as flawless as ever. His bushy black eyebrows stood out against his perfect copper-colored skin. He provided her with a megawatt smile that lightened his whole tough-guy exterior. While his tie-free dress shirt had three buttons undone, his dress pants molded to his toned ass. She assumed he'd left work early to meet her.

"For the record, I thought I would have to fight." Dahl sported a simple jean jacket over a dainty camisole. Truly believing the evening would be a colossal waste of her time, she'd thrown on a pair of jeans and Timberland boots to top off her beat-that-ass ensemble.

"Fight? What's your dating life been like since our breakup?" He offered her his arm.

Tickled that she didn't have to spend her night with the Mavericks' psychopathic quarterback, Shawn Mathers, Dahl grabbed hold of his bulging bicep.

"Where, oh where, are you taking me, Bane Carter?" As she leaned into his hard body, they headed off toward a row of pubs. A good flow of people walked the streets. Since the Cubs were at an away game, most of their fans were in the bars.

"Trust me. You'll like it."

"Says the man who blackmailed me to feed four children."

"Don't exaggerate. The baby can't eat your food... yet." Bane threw her a lopsided grin that he usually held hostage for most of the day.

Bane seemed more relaxed than she had seen him in forever, so Dahl didn't know what to expect. He led her down the cellar stairs of a bar named Sammie's Old Town Tavern.

"Name?" a bouncer positioned in front of a big red door asked.

"Carter."

The man ran his finger down the list on his clipboard. "Got it." He pulled two stickers off a strip and placed them on the backs of their hands. "Past the bar and out the back. Show them your passes." He opened the door for them to enter the small bar.

Bane reached for her hand and used the bulk of his muscled body to maneuver people out of their way. Dahl tried not to do that teenage girly thing, but she couldn't help the squishy sensation that rolled through her body and turned her insides to mush.

Once they'd made it to the back of the bar, they showed another bouncer their stickers. He shoved open the door to allow them access to the backyard area. An even bigger crowd covered a large field, facing a DJ platform and stage. Huge screens showcased cooking stations.

"What is this?" she asked, completely in the dark about what was happening. Dahl slid her gaze up his large frame, finally landing on his face, anxious for him to answer.

"Wait for it," he told her.

While she fought off the urge to pout, a hard techno bass vibrated the grassy field underneath them. Bane squeezed her hand. If anyone knew she had the attention span of a gnat, it was her ex-husband.

"Ladies and gentlemen," the announcer's voice boomed over the music and the enthusiastic crowd, "welcome to the semifinals of Food Fight Club!"

As the contestants filed onto the stage, the audience went wild.

Beyond excited, Dahl danced from foot to foot in front of the gorgeous giant. "I've heard of this," she squealed. "I thought it was, you know, an urban legend."

"We have six contestants to knock out of this round." The announcer ran down the instructions and, behind their prep stations, the contestants put on their chef's jackets. "Our competitors all have their own aesthetics…" The hard sounds of drumbeats introduced two ring girls onto the stage. "Tonight I believe we need some help of the professional variety."

Round lights stationed on the building above flew across the sea of people. "Is there a Baby, a Dahl Baby Hamilton in the house?"

The crowd erupted in manic screams.

"What did you do?" she whispered to Bane as the spinning lights landed on her. Dahl ducked her head in embarrassment for two point five seconds before she threw a wave to everyone.

"Would you, Dahl Baby Hamilton, do us the honors of switching these arrogant chefs' ingredients around to make it damn near impossible for them to cook anything remotely edible?"

The DJ switched from music to the tick-tock sound of a clock which increased the overall suspense of the game. "Of course," she called out.

A boxer-girl grabbed her hand and pulled her onto the stage. Dahl peeked over her shoulder at Bane, who was cheering along with the crowd. He put two fingers to his mouth and whistled.

"Are you ready to ruin these chefs' evening?" The announcer approached her with the microphone and held it toward her. Unable to take her eyes off of Bane, Dahl allowed one of the boxer girls to help her out of her jacket and replace it with a chef's coat. If she had to rate this evening off the bat, she would have to admit it was the best date she'd ever had. There would be no banal chit chat or awkward pauses, and best of all, she didn't have to worry about embarrassing the hell out of herself.

"Will there be tears involved?" Dahl laughed with the audience.

"It wouldn't be Food Fight Club without them!" the announcer screamed above the manic energy.

And with that, Dahl went to work, ruining each chef's plans for success.

Let the games begin…

* * * *

Not one drop of rain fell from the sky, but the streak of lightning overhead told Bane that it wasn't far off. He accepted the funnel cakes from the street vendor and handed one to Dahl. She immediately tore into the sweet treat.

"Mm-m," she moaned.

"How can you still be hungry?" Worried that a spring storm would catch them unaware, he escorted Dahl back to her truck.

"Those chefs only gave us teeny tiny bites."

Most likely high on her ability to reduce grown men to tears, she practically skipped over to her vehicle. He had learned about Food Fight Club from Warner and hadn't been able to pass up the chance to throw his weight around to get them in to view the competition. Sadly, the club was so exclusive that the only name he could use was Dahl's.

"Who knew you had such a psychotic competitive streak?" he asked.

"You did."

They laughed at the truth of it. She had managed to switch Italian, Chinese and Mexican ingredients in such a way that two contestants had been immediately stumped. It had left them no room to finish their dishes. Apparently, that roadblock had been a first in Food Fight Club history.

Dahl turned around to face him when they arrived at her truck. "Thanks… This has been the best hooker date I've ever had."

Dropping his head back, he let off a mighty groan. "It's for my charity, Dahl. If you could refrain from using the term 'hooker', that would be great."

As she held a wayward curl out of her face, she stared back at him with her big doe eyes. He had to fight the urge to take her full lips into his and suck. The wind picked up and blew her sweet scent of vanilla mixed with apricots toward him. He wanted this woman more than he had ever wanted anyone.

"Indecent proposal date? Paid escort? Are either one of those options better?"

"Sure, we'll just print it up on the brochure when we're looking for donations." She threw her head back and laughed. He had always loved that hard cackle from her gut. Once she sobered enough to snort, he finally joined her.

"Are you going to be okay? A pretty big storm is coming." Her eyes shifted toward the sky.

Familiarity created the strangest dynamic. On one hand, he didn't have to hide the fact that he hated storms, but the raw bareness of his secret left him vulnerable. Bane hated to be in that position with Dahl. "I'm a big boy. I'll be fine."

"Okay," she said. She hit the fob on her key chain and opened the door. "That was stupid fun."

"I'm glad you enjoyed it." Bane's brain begged for him to shut the door but he couldn't move. Since she was no longer obligated to come to his house to cook for the kids, he didn't know when he would see her again.

"What?"

"Huh?" he asked, jolted out of his stupor.

"It looked like you wanted to ask me something."

He shook his head to knock away the overwhelming urge to beg her to come home with him. "See you, Dahl."

She tilted her head to the side before she granted him a sweet smile. "Bye, Bane."

He shut her door and waited for her to drive off. One thing he knew above all else. He couldn't afford the distraction of Dahl Baby Hamilton in his life...not again.

Chapter Ten

The hard rain from the storm pelted against the windowpanes in her loft. After she'd left her date with Bane, the storm had finally cut loose.

Above her head, Dahl's chandelier flickered. She snapped pictures of her dessert creations against the large church door that she had fashioned into a table. The tiny strawberry shortcake popped against the background of the detailed wood design. She prayed the storm wouldn't knock out the lights. As she worked, she did her best to dissect the events of the night. That her ex-husband was responsible for one of the best dates she'd ever had unsettled her.

Once her publisher had supplied her with the go-ahead for the book concept, they would hire a stylist to replicate the meals.

As thunder rumbled outside, Dahl took a step back to get a better angle, then the lights shut completely off.

"Great." Two huge scented candles were on top of her hall table. Dahl fumbled around in the dark until she made it to the drawer for something to use to light them. A loud knock at her door forced her to jump back.

"Shit." Not expecting anyone, Dahl felt around for the matches until her hand bumped into them, and she quickly lit the candles. Dressed in nothing but a girly chemise, she suddenly felt exposed.

Dahl grabbed her blue jean shirt off the couch, shrugged it on and tiptoed to the door. Maybe someone from one of the other lofts was in trouble. She looked out of her peephole, but could only make out a large silhouette.

"Dahl, it's me."

Unlocking the door, she cracked it open. Relief flooded through her body at the sight of Bane.

"Are you going to leave me out here?" Leaning in, he pushed his face inches away from hers.

"That depends." For weeks they had rotated around each other with that tug of tension pulling them closer. If she let him in, Dahl wanted his reason to be crystal clear. "What do you need, Bane?"

He took a deep breath before running his hand over his short-cut waves. "I'm standing outside the door of the woman who left me damn near eighteen years ago… I'm definitely in need of something."

It was the closest she would ever get to an admission of interest from him, so she took a step back.

Bane entered the loft, slamming the door behind him. "After all these years, you still do those lacy thingies," he growled.

"Baby dolls, teddies or lingerie?" Being stuck with men in the kitchen all day, Dahl didn't want her femininity to suffer under the weight of her male-dominated career. Her obsession with baby doll lingerie had begun in college. "You can take your pick of names."

"Whatever you call them, it's not helping me talk myself out of this." Bane continued his forward momentum toward her.

"The point of no return was right before you knocked."

"No shit," he hissed. Scooping her up into his arms, he brushed his lips against hers. "If you'd only left sooner…"

"But I didn't," Dahl whispered into his mouth. "Now what?" He grabbed a handful of her ass and hiked her high onto his waist. She wrapped her legs around his big frame, causing an ache of need to shoot through her body. He pulled her shirt from her arm and she shrugged out of the other sleeve, allowing it to fall to the floor.

Another round of thunder rumbled the earth, and the frenetic pace with which Bane was attacking her ratcheted up a notch. He pushed the strap to her teddy off her shoulder.

When he slipped his tongue into her mouth, she sucked on it. He tasted of vodka, pineapple and freesia. The strange drink the bartender had created for the fundraiser was divine on Bane's lips.

While he devoured her mouth, he ran his hard hand over her breast. She hissed at the feel of his touch.

He maneuvered around her coffee table but bumped into a chair. Thankfully, he didn't drop her. For a big man, he had amazing grace.

As he rolled a nipped between his fingers, he pulled away from her lips. "Still like the hard fuck first?"

When Bane slipped his finger into her wet opening, Dahl moaned.

"I'm surprised you remember after so many—"

Cutting off her smart comment, he dropped her on top of her window bench.

As she laughed at his audacity, Dahl hiked her foot onto the bench and inched her way backward.

Licking his lips, Bane unzipped his pants and stalked her path until she hit the large pillow behind her. "I'll take that as a yes." He shoved his pants down and grabbed his cock. Stroking his huge length, he stared at her. Agonizing seconds slipped by before he pushed into her willing body.

Dahl hissed.

"You good?" He held himself up by the window ledge above her.

"Uh-huh." Bane captured her moan between his lips. Moving slowly at first, she adjusted to his sweet rhythm. Intense heat fueled her. She needed to bottle the emotional swell that attacked her every nerve and bask in the sweet warmth of it.

Bane sped up. Grabbing her thigh, he plowed into her pussy. "Oh fuck!" she screamed. The explosion she'd wanted to hold off attacked her in a multitude of intoxicating waves. Arching her back, she moaned as he rolled his tongue over her nipple.

Sinking into the pain and pleasure of his cock, she hit the peak of the quickest orgasm she'd had in her entire life. While surges of heat rolled through her body, he pushed her leg back, working deep inside her pussy, and shuddered out a groan.

Chapter Eleven

The storm finally stopped. A slow shower of rain tapped against her windows. Dahl lay limp on her custom-made bench, listening to Bane knock around in her loft. Positive that he'd broken more than one piece of furniture, she willed herself to get up to find the flashlight, but she didn't have the strength to move.

"Be careful. I broke something dainty in the bathroom." When he pressed a towel between her legs, Dahl sucked in a breath. Tender, she welcomed the heat. "Sorry." He captured her lips, probably to make up for the sins he'd committed against her body moments before.

The lights flickered back on. Before Dahl could brazenly open her legs and coax him into her pussy again, Bane stood up.

"Whoa!" He checked out her loft. "The guys on my team don't ball like this. Holy shit, are those baby cakes!" Bane walked into the kitchen. He plucked a strawberry cake from the table and popped it into his mouth.

"Cookbook ideas," she told him, while she soaked in the muscled contours of his hard body.

He studied one of the twenty Polaroids she had laid out on the table. Recipes that made the first cut got a hard copy, but the rest stayed in her phone until the publishers provided her with the final edit.

"This is good," he muttered about the dessert. "Almost better than Grandma May's. If only she could rise from the dead and sue you."

"Ms. Mable gave me permission to use any of her recipes, so if you try to sue me, Mr. Carter, you won't have a leg to stand on."

"I bet you didn't get that in writing," he grumbled with a spark of humor, popping another treat into his mouth. Dahl laughed. She'd forgotten how talkative he was after a game or sex. The usual strong, silent beast had lots to say once he got a good shot of adrenaline to his veins.

"Yep, Ms. Mable knew you weren't shit and wrote her consent down on the rum cake card." Bane's grandma had been able to cook her ass off. Dahl had to admit that she hadn't truly known anything until Ms. Mable had come into her life. She'd changed her major then from business marketing to restaurant management and culinary science, which had kick-started her ridiculously lucrative career.

"I haven't had her rum cake since she died." Dahl couldn't tell if the wistful expression that shadowed across his face had anything to do with his memories from childhood or the last strawberry cake he'd shoved into his mouth.

"Got numbers two and six lying around?"

Dahl squinted at the Polaroids he held up of a banana nut loaf and a mini crumb cake. "I think I can work something out." She didn't have the ingredients for the banana bread, but she could whip up the crumb cake in a fairly short amount of time.

"Good." He wiped the cream from the corner of his mouth. "It will be the equivalent of a shot of an energy drink later. Now where the fuck is your bed?"

As her gaze slid down his body, landing on his now-raging hard-on, the sound of a boxing bell ringing vibrated in Dahl's head. Before she had let Bane into her apartment, she had been a huge advocate of no sex with an ex. However, at the moment, Dahl failed to see the problem. Her body craved his touch, and whatever the fallout, bad vibes or regret, she was fully prepared to deal with it.

* * * *

Spring showers turned into a dreary drizzle. Bane braved the irritating weather to pick up breakfast.

"Walk of shame, huh, and no one recognized you?"

He set the food bag on the table and glanced up. Dahl leaned over the railing of her upstairs balcony. Soft curls fell onto her beautiful face and the oversized shirt she wore buckled open, allowing him a good peek of her breast. Already semi-hard, he waited for the appearance of a nipple.

"First off, men don't do the walk of shame."

"Are you sure about that?" She laughed.

"Positive. We're card-carrying members of the 'hit it and quit it' club." He nodded toward the bag. "Food's getting cold."

"Yeah!" She clapped. While she walked down her stairs to join him, Bane took the cartons and laid them out.

"I swear that shirt looks familiar. Did you seriously keep it all these years?" Worn through at the elbows, it accentuated her curves.

"It's my favorite." She accepted the box he passed to her. "Where are the kids?"

"Ester took the baby and Cady to church. The rest are at sleepovers or tournaments." He shrugged out of his leather suit jacket and placed it across the seat next to him. "Oh, I grabbed this." He tossed the *Sun-Times* newspaper into her lap. "I'm guessing you won't be going back to the restaurant anytime soon?"

"Wow, slow news day." She picked up the paper and read the article.

"Looks like you also gave me an out… I forgot how petty you could be when you're mad." As he poured maple syrup over his French toast, Dahl grabbed a piece of bacon and took a bite. "Thank you," he said.

"No prob." Dahl smiled before she went back to the paper. Bane took a forkful of their omelet and let her read uninterrupted. He'd already scanned the article while he'd waited for their order.

In the sweetest way possible, his ex-wife had explained to the reporter that she'd had a great few months at the restaurant. Confident that she had left First Down in great hands with the new executive chef, she needed time to work on other projects. Dahl had promised the reporter that the restaurant's business projections would do better than expected and would no longer need the Maverick's GM to finance them.

Bane pushed another box filled with food in front of her. Unless things had changed from years ago, Dahl liked to graze. He didn't bother to plate anything. She would take what she wanted.

"Now that you have free time —" he started.

"Don't you think blackmailing me once was enough, Bane Carter?"

"Trust me, Hamilton. This will benefit you." He reached over and held a fork full of French toast near her lips. Putting down the paper, she took a bite.

"This is good."

"A greasy spoon down the street, great food. Maybe with your highfalutin' credentials, you can go down there and save them, too."

"Hardy-har-har. You got jokes." When Dahl put her foot on the edge of his chair, he immediately dropped his gaze. All he need was a whiff of her pussy and breakfast would be over. Unfortunately, she had on a dainty pair of panties that were blocking his path. After talking his dick down, he cut off a chunk of her pancakes.

"I'm still stuck with a lousy nanny and no cook."

"Bane," she growled.

"Hear me out." He chewed on the fluffy goodness. Reaching for her smooth chocolate leg, he pulled it onto his lap. "You were probably using the restaurants for your… What's that called…a test kitchen?"

"Check you out." Dahl mock gasped.

He rubbed the arch of her foot and waited for her endorphins to kick in. Once he heard her moan, he continued. "My whole life isn't football."

Her eyebrows shot up. "Since when?"

Determined not to be sidetracked, he pushed forward. If they moseyed down that path, then there would be no more good vibes. The previous night, Bane had realized that he not only wanted Dahl, but he also needed her. "Unlike your loft, my house has amazing light all day and a big enough kitchen for you to make several dishes at a time."

"And all I have to do is-s-s…"

"Cook, of course—at least until you find another show, book, program, et cetera, et cetera." Pulling her closer, he split the space between them by half. Inches away from her face, he smelled the syrup on her lips.

"Okay, okay," she muttered. "But do you really think you can afford me?" He opened his mouth, but she held up her hand to stop him. "Even though you bid a ridiculous amount of money on me."

"It was either that or have you stab my quarterback to death, which is a lose-lose for me." Bane smirked. "To be honest, I just wanted to *Indecent Proposal* the shit out of you." He knew Dahl always appreciated the truth.

"Is twenty-five thousand dollars all I'm worth?" she whispered seductively into his mouth. While he cursed the barrier of thin fabric that covered her pussy, Bane caressed his way up her toned leg.

"Nah, baby, so much more, but withdrawing early caused you to incur penalties on your interest." The sweet kisses he placed on her neck didn't stop her from throwing her head back to laugh. One thing was for sure. He could count on Dahl to see the humor in their epic break-up.

* * * *

The annoying screech of the timer pierced the air. Dahl turned the pot pies in the rack to help them cook evenly before she shut the oven door. As she reached over to reset the clock for fifteen minutes, Sebastian cooed in his Babybjörn carrier .

"Watch *Paw Patrol* with me, Dolly?" Cady bounced up and down on her tiptoes.

"Did you pick up your toys?"

"Ah-h-h—"

"I'll watch with you, honey." Chelle stepped into the kitchen behind the four-year-old. While she played with the little girl's ponytail, she stared coldly at Dahl.

"No." Cady knocked Chelle's hand away. "I want Dolly to do it."

"Toys," Dahl whispered.

"Okay." The little miss spun on her heels and bounded up the stairs.

"What are you doing here?" Chelle hissed.

Dahl pulled off the oven mitts with a snort. "Oh shit, you're serious."

The petulant nanny put her hands on her hips. "Last I heard, you were let go."

"I'm not sure if you're aware of the time, but it's after noon."

"Mr. Carter knows I had an appointment this morning. That's why I'm late."

Chelle's crazy stalker glare didn't intimidate Dahl in the least. Instead, she tilted her head, confused at the young woman's obvious psychopathic tendencies. "Okay, girl... I got me a date with *Paw Patrol*."

Attempting to fight sleep, the baby sucked on his fist. Dahl brushed her lips across his head and tried to slip past the unstable woman.

"The agency said my assignment has two weeks left." Chelle grabbed her arm before she could leave. "Trust me. I'm going to spend every waking moment trying to convince Bane to keep me."

Finding her attempts at intimidation laughable, Dahl snatched her arm out of her grasp. "Cool… Keep me posted."

Gently bouncing the baby with each step, she made her way up the stairs. Soon Sebastian would be asleep and she could put him down. Ester usually watched the infant, but that morning, the older woman had seemed under the weather. Dahl wanted to check on her before lunchtime but had gotten held up by the worst nanny on earth.

As she walked by Alana's room a pitiful melody of adolescent angst forced Dahl to stop. After lightly tapping on the teen's door, she didn't wait for a reply. She grabbed the knob and entered. "Hey there, bacon, what's shaking?"

Alana hurriedly wiped at her face. "Nothing." She sniffled.

"Dolly, *Paw Patrol!*" Cady bounded into her big sister's room.

"Get out." Red-faced and with a quiver in her voice, Alana demanded the little girl leave. "Nobody invited you."

Even in the thick of the sibling commotion, the baby's eyes drooped. Ready for the littlest member of the Carter clan to go to sleep, Dahl took a seat on the girl's bed. Once she got done hissing teenage words of voodoo at her sister, Alana would probably need an ear above the age of five to listen to her.

"That dumb girl who took her clothes thinks she wants her stupid boyfriend, so they kicked her out of the club."

"It's not a club, you idiot."

"Hey." Dahl threw a small pillow at Alana. "Reserve name calling for people not related to you." The teenager's gaped mouth expression quickly dissolved into a peal of laughter.

"Fine... I'll call everyone else an idiot, but not Cady."

"Deal. Now what's up?"

After a few minutes of a strange high school tale spun from emotion and silliness, Cady wandered off and the baby fell asleep.

"So Tracy told Brittney that I went off with Mark at the dance, but I only talked to him for a few seconds then went to find the girls, and —"

Dahl held up a hand for her to stop. "First, did you finish that proposal I asked for?"

"Are you even listening to me?" She threw her hands up with a melodramatic sigh.

"It's related."

"Yeah, I just finished it."

"Cool, because the answer to your problem is-s-s..." She drew it out until the girl fell on top of her vanity with a groan. "You need a different gang without looking like you dumped the old ones."

"That's nearly impossible! I'm new."

"Summer is in a few weeks. Start working on it. Talk to some kids you don't usually talk to and get their numbers. Do a little scouting over the break, and while you're doing all that, we'll crank out makeup videos for you to put online."

"So you don't think this will just blow over?"

Dahl got up from the frilly pink bed with a snort. "No... They probably started to hang with you just to make you a pariah in the first place. Tiffany, Iffany —"

"Brittney," Alana corrected her with an eye roll.

"She wanted to keep you close in case you had the potential to become HBIC."

"A what?"

"Head—"

Alana nodded her head toward the door where Cady stood in the hall glaring at them.

"You promised." She crossed her arms and threw her the cutest mad-toddler pout.

"Let me put the baby up and I'll be right there."

"Fine." Cady blew out a breath and stomped away.

"Babe in charge," Dahl finished.

"That's not it." Alana giggled.

"If you knew that, why did you ask?" Dahl stood up, already worn out by the kids.

"I wanted to see if you would say it."

"When you go back on Monday, don't show any cracks—and start to get used to the idea of new friends. Also, Alana?"

"Yeah?"

"They're not good enough to be your friends." Dahl chucked deuces over her shoulder before she headed out of the room. "Lunch in thirty."

"Dolly!"

"Sh-h-h." She headed past the bossy child's room. "Start the DVD and I'll be right there." A holiday she hadn't remembered had given all the kids in the district a day off, which made more work for her. At this rate, she would never finish her book.

"Hey, Ester, how are you doing?" Dahl didn't bother to knock. She didn't want to wake the baby. "Oh crap, Ester!" Dahl rushed to the older lady, who lay on the floor unconscious, and checked her pulse. "Alana, call nine-one-one!" she called out.

"Why?" she hollered back.

"Just do it!" She grabbed Ester's wrist to feel her pulse and found a slight rhythm.

"Oh God, oh God!" As the teenager stood wide-eyed and confused in the hallway, she dropped her phone on the floor. "Oh God!"

"Nine-one-one... What's your emergency?"

The first hiccup from the baby warned her, but it didn't prepare her for the piercing wail of anger. Dahl scrambled for the abandoned iPhone. Hoping she didn't need to call the ambulance for both Ester *and* Alana, she tried to explain to dispatch what had happened.

Chapter Twelve

Bright lights lit the stage. Bane waited off to the side for the rest of the team's draft picks. Everything would turn into a circus of post-interviews, dinners and meet-and-greets with the rookies after the presentation. Bane had no intention of sticking around to witness any of it. He checked his watch for the hundredth time that night.

Ever since they had struck their bargain, Bane hadn't seen Dahl. She had usually slipped out of the house by the time he got home. Determined to catch her, he'd made plans to leave after his recruits were announced. Of course, the ceremony was almost over.

"Winston." The hairs on the back of his neck stood straight up at the sound of his first name. No one ever called him that. Taking a deep breath, he plastered on a smile before he turned around.

"Rachel," he said to ex-wife number two. They'd made it a whopping year and a half, and only that long due to the fact that they barely saw one another. "What are you doing here?"

Once a tall, willowy ex-model, she was now a correspondent from some crappy station he couldn't remember. She puckered her lips for a kiss. Certain that she wanted him to genuflect, instead he brushed his cheek next to hers. "Coop invited me."

"Of course he did." Bane chuckled.

"He wanted me to get exclusives with the new draft picks, shooting them with their families—yada, yada, yada."

Bane was positive that several other high-profile anchors had been available to cover the event, but his boss had settled on his ex-wife. *Message received, old ass.*

"The last season for the Mavericks was a little hairy." Rachel's man-eating smile was tight and wide. "A little birdie told me production still needs someone to be head anchor for their sports division at the station. Longevity, Winston." She wagged her finger at him. "That's the key."

"I'm fine." Annoyed by her presence, he felt very little for her, good or bad. It was a completely different reaction from what he had with Dahl.

"That's generally what people think," she admitted.

A guy with a camera approached them. "We're ready for you, Ms. True." The kid gave him a dirty look before he left them backstage.

Bane smirked. "Still charming the young ones."

"A little crush," she purred. "Nothing more. Now, back to you. When are you going to let go of this little football dream?" She stepped in front of him. 'Too demanding and too clingy' summed up their whole relationship. "Because, as far as I can see, this 'first black GM in the league' experiment has failed."

Rachel had never wanted him in the front office. It didn't offer enough exposure or money for her taste. It was another reason out of a million why they hadn't worked.

"It's a good thing nobody asked you," Bane noted.

The shallow smile didn't match the downward crease near her eyes. "When you're done sinking, call me." She sniffed, sauntering off in a slow, sly manner.

"Should I buy you a drink after that massacre?" a new voice asked.

"If I in any way cared, then yes." Bane laughed at his former teammate. He was happy to see Warner James, and they slapped hands and gave each other a half hug. His old friend was an agent for the pros.

"Shit, I was going to make you pay for my drink at that fancy restaurant you own with Trey."

"Trying to shove that knife a little deeper?" Bane shook his head. Warner knew about the hole he'd dug for himself with the restaurant.

"That's the least of your problems, my friend. There are some campfires that are about explode to Smokey Bear proportions."

"Nike wants me to leave the league and sign an old timer's endorsement deal worth millions?" Bane joked.

"Shit, I wish," Warner said wistfully. "Do you know what my commission would be?"

"I can only imagine."

"There's some stuff I heard that you're going to want to get in front of. I'll hit you up, okay?" Warner chucked him on the arm. "In the meantime, I got a guppy on the hook who doesn't know any better."

"Get 'em young," Bane joked.

"Man, at least I break them in slow. These new agents fuck them with no lube — or even condoms, for that matter. It's just a real rough ride." Warner laughed.

Bane nodded goodbye before he reached for his phone. He hadn't seen Dahl in almost a week. Having been forced to put his cell on vibrate due to the ceremony, he glanced at the screen. His chest tightened at all his missed calls. Without waiting to shake hands with their final draft pick, he hit voicemail and headed for the exit.

"Winston Bane Carter?" Autograph seekers swarmed the backdoor to the convention center. Bane pushed through the crowd that waited to catch a glimpse of someone famous. "Can you sign this? I'm a big fan."

As he put the phone between his ear and shoulder, he scribbled his name at the bottom of an old *Sports Illustrated* cover that featured him. Before he passed his autograph back, the guy jerked the top part of the magazine away.

"Winston Carter, you've been served." The man disappeared in the crowd. Bane stopped himself from snatching the little asshole back to make him explain the custody papers he had clutched in his hands.

"Bane, we had to call an ambulance. Ester passed out and she was admitted to —" A roaring freight train of pain roared through his skull. *"She'll be at Northwestern Hospital."*

"Fu —" he hissed, barely able to keep the expletive from leaving his mouth. Bane unlocked his truck from his key fob and rushed to the car.

"Mr. Carter!" someone called out from behind him.

Ignoring the person, he opened his car door and jumped into his truck. Whatever they needed could wait. Bane shoved his key into the ignition and stepped on the brake before he peeled out of the convention center's parking lot.

Speeding most of the way, Bane arrived at the hospital in record time. However, just as he'd arrived, his assistant called to inform him Ester had been released. Changing course, he went straight to her retirement village.

Twenty minutes later, he pulled his car into Ester's parking lot and got out. Not overly impressed with the building's layout, he found it clean but small.

He was accosted the minute he stepped into the complex's lobby. The tiny security guard attempted to frisk him. He had to promise the woman four season opener tickets to convince her not to call the cops.

Positive he had been hustled by the guard but not really caring, he made his way into the elevator. Since Bane wasn't big on enclosed spaces, the rickety cab he had to endure moved the meter of his crappy mood closer to purely grouchy.

As Bane stepped out of the death trap, he took a deep breath and walked down the narrow hallway. Hoping he wouldn't wake Ester from much-needed rest, he stopped at her apartment door and knocked.

"Come in," she called out in a weak voice.

Bane grabbed the knob and opened the door.

"If you wanted a day off, all you had to do was ask," he told the one constant in his life. Illuminated by low light, Ester lay on the couch, covered with a brightly-colored afghan.

"And you still wouldn't have given it to me." She laughed.

If Bane had felt large in the hallway, he felt absolutely enormous in her cozy apartment. Everything seemed too cramped and small for one normal-sized human being, let alone a giant with his large frame.

"Pop a squat, Bane, and get whatever it is off your chest."

Photographs of her family covered the walls — three boys and a girl he knew she'd raised by herself. However, that summed up most of what he knew about the small but mighty woman's personal life. For some odd reason, he suddenly regretted that he didn't know more about Ester Samuel.

Bane sat on the flower-patterned chair that could barely fit his left ass cheek comfortably. "Why didn't you tell me?"

The frail woman sighed. Everything he didn't want to admit out loud stared him in the face. Ester was sicker than he'd initially believed — and not with the common cold.

"Because you have enough on your plate. You didn't need me making things worse."

"Let me be the judge of how much my plate can handle." They sat in silence. It was the first time all day he'd managed to catch a breath. Shifting his weight to relieve the pressure on his ass cheek, he finally gave up and accepted the numb tingles of pain. "Move into the house with me and the kids."

"No siree Bob." She pierced her lips and rapidly shook her head.

"To say I'm worried about you is an understatement."

"Bane—"

"Hear me out." He held up his hand to silence her. "I will promise you allocated private time with no kids, and you can come back to your apartment on the weekends."

Ester fixed her eyes on a picture of her family that sat on the coffee table. From what little Bane knew, her kids were scattered all around the US in different stages of adulting. While she silently made up her mind one way or the other, he sat quietly, waiting for her answer.

"On two conditions," she said after some time had passed. "First, you have to get rid of that horrendous nanny the second her contract is up, and second, stop trying to piss off your ex-wife."

Bane narrowed his gaze at the strange but brilliant woman across from him. "How did you know?"

"Old doesn't mean senile."

"I never said as much, but I'm pretty sure Dahl didn't tell you we used to be married."

"She didn't have to. Nobody with her type of career would walk into the shitstorm you've created unless they cared deeply about you—not even a groupie. Try not to mess it up this time."

"Why are you so sure it was me who screwed it up?"

"Unless the infinitely stubborn Bane Carter has had a personality adjustment in the last twenty-four hours"—she rubbed her thumb across her fingers and winked—"I'd place money that the break-up was your fault."

"So the answer is yes, you're going to move in with us?" Bane chuckled at her semi-accurate analysis of his failed relationship with Dahl.

"Soon… but only if you can act right, my boy. Only if you can act right."

Chapter Thirteen

As soon as he walked into the house, whimsical music from the Dolby surround sound hit him. Bane shut the front door and took a look around. Several amazing smells emanated from the kitchen.

Loosening his tie, he went down the spiral staircase to the media room. After his second divorce, the house had seemed too big. Now it almost seemed too small, as Bane stepped into his theater and took in the sight of a room full of kids.

"Please tell me that's not sticky goo on my awesome, custom-made leather seat." He leaned against the door and fought back a smile. Wall-to-wall kids covered every inch of the place. An abandoned pizza box lay on the floor near a knocked-out Cady and some random kid he'd never met before.

"Sorry." Dahl stood, and the blanket that covered her waist fell to the ground, allowing him good glimpse of her awesome abs. "We threw an impromptu sleepover."

"Hence the extras." Each of his kids had a double. A good basketball team littered the room. He nodded for her to follow him. Dahl gingerly stepped around the sleeping kids and accompanied him out of the door.

"Whoa." Bane jumped back from the possible collision with the night nurse.

"Sorry, Mr. Carter. So sorry," she apologized profusely around a mouthful of a mini hot dog that looked amazing.

"It's cool, Maria."

"I can get the baby and go up," the little woman said. She appeared nervous around him, but most people did. His six-foot-seven frame did little to put people at ease.

"Are you kidding?" Dahl pushed her into the room. "Finish the movie, but more importantly, make sure no one wanders."

"Yes?"

"Yes," she assured her. Dahl grabbed his arm and shoved him toward the stairs.

"What the hell, Dahl? You're never supposed to get them wet."

"Two out of six aren't gremlins." His ex-wife laughed.

"Who the hell are you underestimating? Just give it time." They walked into the kitchen, farther away from the blasting sounds of Harry Potter fighting something or the other that was on. "How can they sleep through that?"

"Loud movies work better than NyQuil on kids. How's Ester?"

"Cancer. She's been going to treatments with church folk when they're available. I guess you were right."

"I wish I hadn't been."

"She's having a hard time keeping anything down except your cooking," he told her.

Dahl placed her hand on her chest and batted her eyes.

"Don't let it go to your head. You use a lot of spices."

Stopping dead in her tracks, she glared at him as if he'd sprouted two heads.

"Fine," he relented. "You're an awesome chef, but don't start feeling yourself. Anyway, I'm having her move into the house as soon as she is up to it."

"I thought she wanted to retire down South?"

"Yeah, I nixed that idea. She'll get better care here." He smirked at her. "Besides, who's going to feed her?"

"Softy," Dahl cooed.

Grabbing one of her mini hot dogs off a tray, he shoved it into his mouth. "Mm-m." He moaned at the burst of flavors. "Cookbook contenders?"

"I'm not sure yet."

When she turned toward the cappuccino maker, he devoured the sight of her full ass. "Let me guess." Bane reached for a baby slider next. "You're making random recipes because you don't have a theme — What?"

Dahl shook her head, staring at him with a familiar expression that was a mix between surprise and annoyance. He didn't know which one he took more pleasure in.

She said, "Why can't you just be —?"

"A dumb jock." He winked. "Then you wouldn't be standing across from me right now, which brings me to my next question."

Dahl steamed the milk in a container.

"Stay at the house… It's crazy for you to drive all the way back to the city so late."

Dahl poured the hot drinks into cups. "What kind of message would that send?" She turned around to set them down and—using a toothpick—began to play in the foam.

Bane grinned at the frothy football she made in his cappuccino before she slid it over. "Hopefully the type to convey that I don't give a shit what anyone thinks." He blew on his coffee. Once he felt it cooled off enough, he took a sip. A soft wave of pleasure washed over him from the smooth but strong flavor. "Especially to anyone who doesn't pay my bills."

Dahl's big brown eyes connected with his. She seemed to study him for a moment. Landing on some answer in her head, she nodded and turned back to the machine to clean it.

The day that had started off hectic then had careened into crap somehow tilted itself upright. He was seriously afraid the good part had everything to do with Dahl. It was a feeling he didn't need or want. In the time they had been apart, he'd done his best to never think about her at all.

Since he wanted to keep all introspective thoughts at bay, he decided he needed a little help in that department—something else to focus on. Bane walked around the island separating them and stood behind her to get a good grip on her shapely hips.

"Mr. Carter…" Dahl said.

"Hm-m?" Moving her hair out of the way of her neck, he placed his lips there.

"What are you doing?"

Bane didn't believe actual words were necessary. He drew his hands across the front of her tank to cup her awesome double-Ds.

"Bane." Dahl leaned back into his lips while he swirled his fingers around her nipples.

As he unbuttoned her jeans, he moved to that space between her shoulder and her neck to kiss her.

"What about the full house?" she asked.

He didn't bother to reply. Instead, he slipped his hand into the waistband of her jeans. Moving past the lacy fabric of her underwear, he sought out her pussy.

Grabbing her by the crown of her beautiful, curly hair, he pulled her head back with one hand and circled her clit with the other.

"Mm-m," she groaned.

Bane dipped his finger into her slit to pull in and out of her tight opening. While he continued to move inside her, he continued thumbing her nub. It was just a matter of minutes before she bucked against him.

When Dahl petered off into those sweet puffs of breath, he knew he had her right where he wanted her.

Turning her around, he brushed his lips against hers. She opened and circled her tongue against his before she panted out the remains of her orgasm.

His cock was hard, super hard. Bane picked Dahl up with ease and carried her into the laundry room. Not in the least bit surprised to see a ton of clothes piled on the floor, he kicked them to the side. For some odd reason, the kids were allergic to anything that resembled an actual chore.

Bane shut the door with his foot. With his lips still locked with hers, he set her down to unbutton his pants. Dahl hurriedly pushed hers over her hips.

Her exposed breasts peeked out of the top of her tank, and Bane took a step back. The pornographic sight of Dahl made him drool. Completely naked would work better, but a house full of people nixed those plans. He jerked his cock in his hand and envisioned all the filthy things he wanted to do to his ex-wife.

Using the bulk of his body, he backed her into the dryer.

Strong in her own right and sexy as hell, Dahl didn't need to be coddled. He let go of his cock long enough to lift up her leg, then he pushed into her slick folds.

He moaned. Bane kept his eyes locked with hers.

He strengthened his hold on her leg and sucked on her neck as he rocked into the sexy chef's body.

"Oh... Oh..." Dahl groaned out. A blissful look swept across her face and her pouty mouth fell open. "Shit!" she cried softly and began to match him thrust for thrust. He continued riding her pretty pussy into oblivion until her inner walls clutched his cock in another orgasmic spasm.

Dropping her head back with a sigh, she went limp in his arm. Happy to join her in sated bliss, he increased his speed and pumped every bit of his juice into Dahl Baby Hamilton's awesome body.

Chapter Fourteen

Dahl woke up with a big sexy ex-football player nuzzling her neck. "Argghh," she groaned.

"Yeah, I blew your back out last night," Bane whispered. "That's why you're facedown in the bed."

She tried to sit up, but her muscles revolted against her attempts and went to jelly.

"Come on, sexy. We've got shit to do." Bane got out of the bed. He pulled the blinds back, allowing the sunlight to chase the comforting darkness from the room. "It's nice outside."

She slid under the covers with a hiss before he pulled the sheet from her body and slapped her on the ass. "Like what?" she muttered, dizzy from her sex headache. Hopefully, the man hadn't done any real damage to her back.

"Whatever you were going to do, but now with help—or at least company. I've got to bring Cady and the baby."

"Bane Carter, don't tell me you've got free time on your hands?" She patted around for the covers, but he must have pulled them too far out of reach.

"Actually, I don't, but with no good nanny and who-the-hell knows where the other one is to even fire her, I have unexpected free time."

Finally giving up on sleep, she flipped onto her back. Wrapped in nothing but a towel, Bane threw her that amazing smile.

"Anything I want?" she asked.

"I'm yours." He winked at her. "Well, yours and the kids…"

"Farmers' market."

"Shit," he chuckled. "Get ready."

* * * *

Rows and rows of fresh fruit and vegetables covered more than a two-block radius within the downtown area. Dahl could spend the whole day at the farmers' market, but she knew Bane had his limits.

She watched him standing in front of the magician with an expression of pure disgust on his handsome face, cradling the baby in the carrier. Enthralled by the kiddie entertainment, Cady sat in front of the man who'd earned Bane's death glare. He had never been one for mimes or clowns. Apparently, she could add magicians to that list.

Once she grabbed the rest of the ingredients for the week's menu, they could finally leave and put the big man out of his misery.

Dahl reached to grab the fresh basil from the basket, accidentally bumping into the person next to her. "Oh sorry, I— Mel?" she asked. Her cousin looked unrecognizable. Her usual flawless face had been scrubbed clean of makeup and her hair looked more like a bird's nest on top of her head. With a wicked scowl on her face, her cousin yanked her hand away from the herbs.

"Hey, what's up?" Dahl asked.

"Don't 'hey' me," Melanie grumbled.

"O...kay." Taken aback by the appearance of her cousin, Dahl shook her head and made a grab for the basil again. This time Mel snatched it from her grip and threw it on the ground. "What the hell is wrong with you?" Dahl asked, now completely confused by the woman's attitude.

"Thanks to you, most of the staff has walked out," Melanie growled.

"Why me? Don't you have an inept husband or manager you can blame?" Dahl moved on to the garlic. Ticking off the items on the list in her head, she knew she needed that and peppers before she could leave.

"They're not the face of First Down."

"Hm-m... I still don't see how this has anything to do with—"

"Bane." Mel nodded and jerked her thumb toward the area where he stood. "You told the press he was leaving the restaurant business to focus on football—and now everyone is jumping ship."

"To make sure I'm getting this right, you think the demise of your restaurant falls squarely on the shoulders of the two people who tried to help you?" She squinted her eyes in an attempt to dissect the stupidity that was obviously rattling around in her cousin's head.

"Trey was the one who thought it would be a good idea to have you come out here. From what I can tell, we were the ones doing you the favor after your shitty show failed, not the other way around."

Dahl laughed a hard belly roar that ended with a snort. "Okay, girl, thanks. I appreciate the opportunity to dig your ungrateful ass out of a hole…again." She grabbed a bag of garlic and put it in her basket.

"What do you think playing house with him is going to do, get you another show?" Melanie pushed her face closer. The usually put-together social butterfly appeared worn out. Finally working, for once in her life, had dimmed her shine, and Dahl couldn't have been more amused by the sight of it. "How about your fertility issues?" Melanie added. "I can't imagine him sticking around much longer after he finds out your shit's dried up."

The urge to snatch her cousin by the neck and choke the crap out of her rolled through Dahl. They were no longer kids, so she couldn't react to her cousin's childish taunts by throat-punching her. She had always hoped Melanie's 'knocking on forties' ass would grow up.

Family or no family, that idiot has just officially burned her last bridge with me. "See? This is where you've got me fucked up. Unlike you, I don't need someone to save me. You can sit here and downplay my accomplishments all you want, but I didn't need that assist. *You* did." While making sure not to raise her voice or change her tone, Dahl planted a fake smile on her face. To draw a crowd would provide her idiot cousin exactly what she wanted—attention. "And when Trey leaves you for that asshole manager you think is your friend, don't call, text or even look in my general fucking direction."

Simmering with unleashed rage, she didn't bother to inspect the peppers on her way past. Instead, she grabbed the first three she saw and threw them into the basket, along with the basil. Tempted to lob every single pepper at her idiot cousin's head, Dahl hurried to the cashier.

From this point forward, Melanie better stay well away from me, if she knows what's good for her.

A drastic change had come over Dahl. Somewhere between the terrible magician and the even cornier puppeteer, he'd caught wind of her cousin's unexpected appearance. If Cady hadn't been on the verge of a meltdown, he would have left as soon as that crazed expression shuttled across Dahl's face. Having been on the receiving end of that look a time or two, he knew what would happen next. From his vantage point, he could tell that Melanie's skinny ass would hit the ground in a matter of seconds.

Once they got back to the house, the kids had kept him busy until he'd managed to get them down for a nap. Bane grabbed two glasses and opened the wine cooler underneath the chef's island, picking out a sweet wine for her, then he headed upstairs.

Counting himself lucky with the two little ones asleep and the others still out for the day, he was in serious need of a freaking nanny. He made his way down the hall and into his room. She was a creature of habit, so he knew Dahl's favorite drug.

Tapping on the half-open bathroom door with the bottle, he pushed it the rest of the way open with his foot. Wife number two had picked most of the features in the house, but before any of it could be implemented,

115

she'd left, which had allowed Bane time to scrap everything the lunatic had wanted.

Walking into the dimly lit room, he stepped toward the enormous whirlpool tub. "Wife number two ordered a clawfoot tub for the master."

Pulling the washcloth away from her face, Dahl looked at him with red-rimmed, puffy eyes, and he could tell she'd been crying. "There's no way you would fit."

"Yeah, that's why we're divorced." Bane took a seat on the third step. "I knew it was over after that." She graced him with a small smile that didn't convince him of anything. Since the farmers' market, the sadness that had seeped into her eyes had appeared to linger.

"Why haven't you ever been married? I mean, after us?" Bane pried. He pulled the stopper out of the wine bottle and poured them both a glass before handing one over to her.

"Too busy, too ambitious… It never came up."

"Or did you avoid it?" he asked.

Dahl took a sip of wine. "Probably. Let me guess… You heard my fight with Melanie."

"I caught the tail end of it. I was afraid you were going to kill her, so I cut short the unadulterated kiddy torture with those whack-assed clowns."

This time her smile pushed her cheeks a little higher. "Uh, yeah… I have a twisted ovary and the other one is damaged. So voilà, I'm broken." Tears slipped down her face and Dahl quickly swiped at them with the back of her hand.

"When did you find out?"

"When I was in my late twenties."

After our divorce. He let out a sigh of relief. At least he didn't have to get mad about her holding back pertinent information, especially when he had his own secrets he'd never shared. By that time, Dahl had been long gone. He didn't want to push her, but perhaps he should have prefaced the question in a different way. "Is that what kept you from ever settling down with one of those shady-ass Parisian guys?"

"Partly," she muttered over the rim of her glass. "What made you keep getting married?"

"Ouch... I thought twice was the normal amount." Bane drank the wine, which was way too girly sweet for his taste, but he knew Dahl didn't like to drink alone.

"For a football player, you mean?"

"Hey now, I didn't come here for the abuse." Bane pouted.

She laughed.

Finally.

"Once a woman figured out *she* was the side chick and football was the wife, all my relationships failed," he admitted out loud for the first time.

"And kids?"

"They were never on my radar," Bane admitted, a slip of a lie. Since he hadn't wanted any after Dahl, it didn't really matter, especially in light of what she'd shared. "Then bam... I'm forty-one and raising four of them by myself."

"True." She tilted her wine glass in his direction. "In for a penny."

"Yep." He scratched at the stubble on his face. "Everything happens for a reason, I guess. My brother and his wife..." He tapered off. Bane had practically raised Devon and it still hurt like hell to think about him. "It's the only way I can look at this objectively."

"You're still logical to a fault."

True. If nothing else, Bane knew he was pragmatic — except when it came to the sexy woman lounging in his tub. "Want to go out for dinner?"

"What about the kids?"

"No backup, so they would have to come with us. Hey" — he pointed at her funky expression — "one way or another, they'll have to learn how to act in public."

"Sure, dinner's fine...but today's not that day. A pizza will work."

He got up to do her bidding. "Okay, but I'm getting a ton of meat. Oh, and, Dahl" — he rapped his knuckles across the wood door to get her attention — "the one thing you will never be is broken."

Allowing him a slight smile, she put the cloth back over her eyes. "You, Bane Winston, are the meanest, sweetest man I have ever met."

Chapter Fifteen

With summer officially in session, the kids had turned into first-rate goblins. Dahl had their time planned down to the minute. That way, none of Bane's little ducks wandered off. Jarin hung out at the stadium most afternoons, which left her with three kids instead of four.

It took them some time, but they finally got down to a good rhythm. Alana shot videos of Cady helping her to cook kid-friendly meals. They were adorable five-to-ten-minute tutorials. They taped the prep for their vanilla bomb pop explosion. Later they would finish baking the cake and shoot the rest of the video.

"Hey, I made a new friend who has potential, and she wants to pick me up to go to the mall. Can I?" Alana begged.

"Have we met her before?"

"No, but…" Alana shifted from foot to foot.

"Text Bane and ask him."

"We both know what he'll say," Alana whined.

"Give it a shot." As the teenager wandered off with a perfect teenage shoulder sag, she typed away on her phone.

"Uncle Bane is going to tell her no," the munchkin said.

Dahl grabbed a towel and scrubbed the vanilla icing off Cady's face. "Don't worry about it. Her little friend can come here."

Chelle walked into the kitchen. Dahl hadn't seen the nanny in days—and for good reason. Her contract had expired. Positive Bane hadn't renewed it, Dahl didn't let on that there was a problem.

"Go and do whatever cooking things you have to do," Chelle said. "I've got the kids."

"Bane wanted to go over a few things with you," Dahl lied easily. "He'll be back in a half hour."

"Really?" Chelle's face brightened.

"Yeah. If you want, I'll wait. That way you won't have to worry about the kids while you talk with him."

"Okay, cool. I just have to go to the washroom." Chelle disappeared in a flash.

Quickly placing the sour cream vanilla icing in the fridge, Dahl wiped her hands on her apron.

"Go get your stuff." While she pushed the toddler toward the mudroom, Dahl snatched her phone off the counter and texted Alana to meet her at the car in five minutes.

Once she'd made it far enough away, she would alert the security at the gate to get Chelle out of the house. Hopefully, that would work. Something felt seriously off with the nanny and she had no plans to stick around to witness her Lifetime-movie meltdown.

* * * *

Bane walked into the ritzy Northside coffee shop, where bright lights bounced off the floor-to-ceiling marble. It wasn't exactly a spot he would have picked for a business meeting. Warner waved him over to the bar with that white boy Clive Owen swag that women fell for. He took a seat next to the agent.

"What the hell is this?" Bane asked, gesturing at their surroundings.

"Don't tell me you don't like coffee." Warner laughed.

Bane grabbed the frou-frou menu from the brass rack and shook his head. "My fifteen-year-old niece would love this place. What does that tell you?"

"Yeah, well, boutique coffee beans are all the rage. How's First Down?"

"No idea. Trying to find an investor to buy me out."

"Well, it's tanking big time since that sexy chef left. If I were you, I'd get her ass back ASAP or it will look like your brand is hexed."

"It's that bad?"

"It certainly doesn't look good. An international chef ended her long-running, lucrative show just to have this blight on her resume. Like I said…cursed, man."

"Uh, I thought ratings had been down?" Bane muttered. He'd never asked her about the program because he'd assumed it had gotten canceled. But if she'd bailed on a for-sure thing to save her cousin—or even him, for that matter…

Shit! A ball of dread swelled in his stomach.

The server stopped by the counter in front of them. He still didn't know what to order, so he landed on the safest thing he could find. "I'll have a mocha cappuccino, please."

"Two," Warner said. "Trust me. You should buy out your cousin. Winning is a good look for the GM. Also…" He tapped on his phone and slid it across the bar toward Bane. The screen showed Shawn's mugshot, his quarterback having been arrested for assault. "This is one of many. Coop's been B&Bing this shit."

Buying off and burying had become a well-known term in the sports field. "For how long?"

"A while now. The Mavericks might be safe for the time being, but your guy here is going to run into a mess that no one can buy his way out of. Then what?"

Amazed at all the people who continued to save the little imbecile's ass, Bane rubbed his hand across his face. "Thanks for the heads-up." He handed Warner back his phone.

"No prob. But what I really wanted to talk about was the family."

The owner of the Mavericks and his sibling were old money, and they had amassed their wealth through various ventures. They were so well known that the media referred to them as 'the family'. Even though each member had a vested interest in the franchise, the team was Coop's baby. "They're underwater and looking for a way to the surface."

"Are you shitting me?"

"No. They need to unload the team at top dollar. A winning season would be great, but in case it goes bad…"

"They need a fall guy—and that's me."

Warner pointed his fingers at him as if they were guns and pulled the trigger. "Bam." He pretended to fire. "That way they can sell it for what it's really worth and blame the diversity hire for the inevitable cut in price."

"No wonder Coach Moron is still around."

"Yep... That way it won't look like the season will be his fault—or your rapey-ass quarterback's. Nope, it's you, Bane Carter—and with that restaurant going belly up—"

"Gotcha," he cut Warner off. Bane had to give it to Dahl. She'd called it. Trying to bail his cousin out had become one more thing to weigh him down. The server placed their piping-hot cappuccinos in front of them.

"I'll bet you wish that was a beer right about now, don't you?" Warner chuckled.

"You have no idea." Bane fought back the urge to beat Trey and anyone else who got in his way senseless. He grabbed the cup and blew on that much-needed caffeine hit. While his mind shot to the night he'd fucked his ex-wife against the dryer, he tried to figure out how to fix his life.

At least one good thing had happened from this mess—Dahl Hamilton. But how long would she stick around? The question bumped inside his head along with everything else. Determined to tackle one problem at a time, he drank the over-priced coffee. Compared to Dahl's sweet concoction from the other night, it tasted dull.

Shit. Officially screwed, Bane set the cup back down.

* * * *

Summoned to the stadium by the higher ups, Bane figured the reason had to be one of two things and both options were straight trash. Either the front office wanted him to stand at the podium with Coop to deliver the official statement about their skeevy quarterback, or they wanted to fire Bane. Honestly, he hoped it was the latter.

Coop and the coach were in the conference room, along with the entire Mavericks' marketing staff. Apparently several members of the press were waiting for a statement. Bane opened the door to the all-hands-on-deck powwow and stepped into the room.

"Glad you could join us," Coach huffed.

Ignoring the idiot, he leaned against the wall. Since they'd invited him at the very last minute, he hadn't bothered to arrive any sooner than he needed to.

"We have your speech ready." The head of PR tried to pass the paper over to Bane.

"What?"

"You're reading it," Coop informed him. The old ghoul didn't even flinch.

"Hold on." He pushed the paper back toward the head of PR. "That sycophant wasn't my doing. Why isn't Coach sweetening up to the vultures?"

"The Mavericks aren't about finger pointing, Bane. We're in this together, and we need you to take one for the team," Coop scolded him.

"In other words, you're hanging me out to dry. Got it." He accepted the statement from the publicist, who at least had the decency to appear embarrassed. Bane scanned the snow job—and he snorted. If they wanted him to handle it, he'd do so—perhaps not quite like they intended, however. He turned toward the door to his fate.

The media room was jam-packed. Bane stepped onto the podium and took in the crowd. Media veterans who didn't venture out unless a catastrophic event had taken place were seated in the front row.

"Any questions?" He rolled up his sleeves, ready to get muddy. Using one of Alana's favorite quotes, the sports press was *'the worst'*.

"Uh, aren't you going to give us a statement?" Art Newman peeked over his bifocals at his fellow journalists, confused.

"Ask now or forever hold your peace," he told the old, cantankerous man. "You guys have got five minutes."

"Quarterback Shawn Mathers has had quite the bad-boy reputation. These new allegations are the most serious to date. Will the team stand behind him?"

Bane took a deep breath and began. "The front office will be conducting our own investigation into this matter. If we find any evidence supporting the accuser's claims, Shawn will be removed from his position in the Mavericks' organization."

From his vantage point, he could practically see the flames shooting from the top of the coach's peach-fuzz-covered head. The idiot stood in the back of the room with the marketing team. Strangely enough, the five ladies who headed it up appeared relieved.

"Is this protocol?"

"It is now." He pointed at one of the few female reporters in the room. "Brenda…"

"There has always been murmuring about Shawn's exploits. Why would the team keep him when a handful of free agents with better reputations are available for the upcoming season?"

A good question that the Mavericks' stupid coach should have to answer. Bane pinned the red-faced idiot with a blistering stare before he replied.

"Unfortunately, the league in general is more about performance than moral obligation. Since I've been hired as general manager, I'm hoping to change that. Last question."

"We've seen this a million times!" Tina shouted, to beat one of the more crotchety old timers to a question. "The accuser mysteriously drops the allegations and nothing changes. What makes your investigation different?"

"The difference is that I'm in charge now." Officially done, he stepped down from the podium.

As the press shouted questions at him, Bane walked out of the room.

"None of that shit was in the statement," the coach barked. Hot on his heels, the little stooge had the nerve to follow him toward the exit.

Bane turned around to face the little turd who had plotted against him the moment he'd signed on for the general manager position. "To tell the truth, Coach, you're lucky I didn't give up the goods about your boy and your support of him."

Once he'd reached the end of the hallway, he kicked open the stairwell exit and left the man red-faced and sputtering.

* * * *

After the press conference, Bane went back to his office to finish paperwork and pick Jarin up from the stadium. He'd forgotten to text Dahl about dinner but figured she would have told him him to grab something on the way if she didn't want to cook. He turned onto his street.

"What the—?" Lights from fire trucks brightened his entire gated community.

"Uncle Bane, that's *our* house!" Jarin said.

Smoke billowed from the back. He put the truck in park and got out, telling Jarin to stay put until he could get a read on the situation. Gripped by the sight of his place on fire, he headed toward his driveway.

"Hey, hey, wait a minute, sir." A fireman stepped in front of him.

"That's my house." Bane beat back the panic. He had no idea where Dahl and the girls were.

"Sir, I'm Inez Lopez." A stern little woman sidled alongside the fireman. "DCFS." She flipped her badge at him.

"Huh?" He moved toward his house once again, but a cop joined the growing crowd blocking his way.

"We received a call about a case of child abandonment. I'm here to secure the well-being of Jarin, Cady, Sebastian and Alana Carter."

Not too long ago, Bane had broken bodies for a living. Playing football for him had become a brutal art of meditation. Off the field, he couldn't display the slightest bit of aggression or he would be considered a threat. While his insides went crazy, he fought to keep a calm mask in place.

"Where are the other children, sir?" she asked, indicating Jarin, who was still seated in the car.

At a loss for words, he stared at the woman as if she'd grown a second head.

"Did the person who called you give a name—or was it anonymous?" Dahl stepped from the other side of the street with the kids in tow. Nearly buckling to the ground, he grunted out a huge sigh of relief. "Because I'm guessing it was the same crazy chick who set the house on fire."

"Uh, that's confidential," the social worker answered with a stern tone. "And who might you be?"

"The relief nanny," Dahl offered without hesitation. "And here are the rest of the Carter children, safe and sound."

Grim disapproval shuttled across the woman's already-unhappy face. After a moment, she dug into her purse. "This is my card." She handed it over to Bane. "I'll call you in a couple of days to set up a meeting."

Bane waited for her to leave before he whipped around, unbelievably happy to see the little degenerates. "What the hell?"

"Chelle was here." Dahl handed the baby over to him.

"She was acting weird," Alana said. The teenager held Cady's hand while she scrolled through her phone with her other one.

"Burn-down-my-house weird?"

"Apparently you have that effect on people." Dahl chuckled. "I'm sorry. This isn't funny, but damn, Bane...of all the shit luck."

"That's six dollars, Dolly," Cady reminded them of the swear jar.

"When did it go up to six?"

"Remember that day Chelle took that test tray of cookies you baked home with her?" Jarin, who'd suddenly appeared at their side, piped in.

"Oh yeah." Dahl frowned. "I don't think that should count."

Bane shook his head, amazed at how the emotions of pure rage and sweet gratitude could occupy the same space in his mind.

Chapter Sixteen

Two weeks' worth of construction on the kitchen had turned into three and careened dangerously into four. They were living in the guest house until the work was done.

As the oppressive summer heat damn near smothered him to death, Bane stared at the blades of the ceiling fan. Cute and cozy for three people had become downright miserable for a squad of six. Ester had gone back to her place until the house got fixed up and they still had no word on Chelle's whereabouts. Bane was positive the little psycho had tried to burn his house to the ground.

The foreman had promised him that there would only be one more week of this torture. Pretty sure he would lose his mind way before then, Bane got out of bed to get a jump on the bathroom. Since they had to share, he made sure he was always first.

With his job situation murky at best, he had his doubts about Dahl. She'd cut loose on him once before.

What would stop her from doing it again? He took a quick shower. When he stepped back into the master, Dahl was still in bed, but thankfully awake. The walls of the small house seemed to close in on him. "Can you pick Cady up from camp?"

"Huh?"

Well, maybe not that awake.

"I wouldn't be asking but I have an important meeting," he stated in that matter-of-fact tone he knew she hated.

"Sure. I meet with my publisher today, but I can cut out early."

He put on his boxer briefs then stepped into his khakis. "Forget it."

"What?" As she sat up, her teddy stuck to her chest. He glanced away. Morning sex was the one thing he wanted — but the last thing he needed.

"Never mind... I'll figure something out," he snapped while he shrugged into a polo shirt. He wanted air conditioning and his own freaking bed. Bane didn't want to deal with a jacked-up house, an uncertain job situation with four kids and last, but not least, Dahl Baby Hamilton. *The infuriating love of my life.*

He hadn't been this edgy since his football days. Back then, Bane would build up a crazy amount of tension then unleash it on the field. At the moment, it had nowhere to go.

Dahl snatched a magazine from the nightstand to fan herself. "What the hell, Bane? I said I'd do it."

"Are you sure? Because I would hate to mess with your precious schedule."

"What is your problem?"

"Fine." He engaged the clasp on his watch and grabbed his keys. "Pick her up at noon on the dot.

They're closing early." Slamming the drawer to the nightstand, he walked out of the room. Childish maybe, but if she decided leave, he wanted her to do it sooner rather than later.

* * * *

They hated her pitch. Twenty minutes into the meeting, four editors had shown various degrees of visible scowls. Thirty minutes in, a couple of them had mentally checked out and glanced at their phones.

As Dahl's test photos covered the conference table, she tried to convince them that this was the book everyone needed.

"Not to be a complete idiot, but this whole pitch is purely about appetizers, correct?" Tiny Glasses, Thin Eyebrows asked.

"How will people relate to a book full of condensed dishes? America is known for big plates," Severe Bun added.

Drumming her fingers across the surface of the table, Dahl swallowed her smart comment to the edgeless idiot. "Meat, vegetarian and vegan," she answered with a smile.

"Mounds of food on big plates is what this country is known for," Asshole Face muttered, without bothering to take his eyes off his phone.

"Perhaps you can come back with something a bit more cohesive in a few weeks."

"We'll definitely have something for you guys to look at," her agent, Trish Lively, replied.

We? Dahl wanted to breathe fire at her. Officially dismissed, she scooped up her photos and she and Trish walked out of the door with her agent. While they waited for the elevator, she tapped her foot to an erratic beat. Dahl didn't want to give in to childish tantrums in front of everyone.

The doors opened. "Now, Dahl," Trish started, probably in an attempt to beat her to the punch, "it wasn't that bad."

She had never been professionally trashed before. Once they stepped in the elevator and the doors shut, Dahl let loose. "What the fuck was that?" she growled.

"A bump in the road, no big deal. It happens to the best of us." Trish juggled her perfect little black bag and keys in her hand.

"That was some medieval times bullshit, a freakin' blood bath. Why can't we just go to a different publisher?"

Trish finally looked away from the floor numbers above and met her eyes straight on. "Because they're right. The idea sucks, and if we take it somewhere else, we'll get the same reaction."

Stunned speechless, Dahl rode the rest of the way to the lobby in silence. She stepped off the elevator with no intention of speaking to, looking at or working with Trish ever again.

"Hey." The spunky agent grabbed her arm. Resisting the urge to yank it back, Dahl took a deep breath. "I know you have a lot on your plate right now, but you should start taking one thing at a time or your house of cards is going to come tumbling down."

"Anything in particular?"

"The restaurant is having a lot of internal issues. I swear that every five seconds *The Chicago Reader* reports a new chef being hired or another one leaving."

"What does that have to do with me?" Dahl hissed. "It's not even my restaurant."

"Yeah, but you're known for fixing the unfixable, so this kind of looks really bad."

Dahl blew a stray ringlet out of her face. She honestly didn't have a defense. She had known better than to come back to Chicago.

"Either fix that stupid restaurant or go on vacation and come back with some new ideas. I've known you for years, and" — Trish shrugged — "you seem stressed. That's the best word to describe whatever this shit is." The agent made a wide circle with her finger before she patted Dahl's arm, leaving her slack-jawed in the lobby.

The only thing that shook her from her stupor was the clock above the security desk. "Fuck," she said. Beyond late, Dahl made a mad dash toward the garage stairwell.

* * * *

The vein on the side of his head throbbed as Bane tried to calm down.

When he carried Cady to the car, she rested her sticky little-girl head on his shoulder. In the midst of a summer heatwave, his sweat-soaked clothes clung to each and every crevice of his body.

"Uncle Bane, can I have a snow cone when we get home?" she mumbled in a sleepy stupor.

After sitting in the absolute worse meeting of his career, he'd had to leave suddenly to pick Cady up since Dahl hadn't shown. Then he'd then been stuck in serious bumper-to-bumper traffic for thirty minutes. When he'd finally arrived, Cady's camp manager had lost her shit. He'd had to volunteer at three parent days or look for another summer camp. It was just one more thing he didn't need on top of a million on his list.

"Hey, hey, sorry." Dahl ran up to them. "My meeting went long and…"

Opening the back door to his SUV, he strapped Cady into her car seat.

Dahl blocked his path to the driver side. "Look… I got here as fast I co—"

"They threatened to kick the kid out."

"Sorry! I just had the dumbest meeting and—"

He held up his hand, waving her excuse off. "Next week I have a hearing for the kids. Isabella's family wants custody, which means I don't have time for your stuff, too."

"What?" She swiped at the sweat on her forehead with the back of her hand. "But you never told me—"

"Why would I?"

Her eyebrows knitted into a frown. "You must have mistaken me for one of your employees. I don't work for you, Bane."

"And I don't need you to. Remember…it was Melanie who asked you to come back." He turned away from her and opened the door.

"No, but you're the one who asked me to feed your fucking kids, not her." Dahl's skin glowed from the sun, flushed from the heat. She was the one person who could wrap him around her finger, but not today.

Bane grabbed the top of his truck and squeezed the roof of his Land Rover. Too kind, beautiful and many other things, Dahl Hamilton wasn't exclusively his. He refused to do this again. Pushing off the vehicle, he got in. Bane had made enough mistakes concerning his personal life to last him a lifetime. "Don't worry. I've got it from here."

"Do you?" Dahl stepped between him and the door before he could reach for it, enfolding him with her sweet scent of honeysuckle and sandalwood. He was determined to fight off the warm sensation that took over his soul whenever she was near. "Because from where I'm standing, you're drowning and I was the only one throwing you a life preserver." She flicked her hand dismissively in his direction. "Good luck, Bane."

Dahl turned around and walked away. Again.

Chapter Seventeen

Done with anything that didn't resemble a beach and running a tab of fruity drinks, Dahl made plans to leave Chicago. Not sure where she wanted to go, she poured herself another glass of merlot and did a little recon on destinations.

For the past two days, she'd looked for different publishers. She had enough clout in the industry to bypass the query process. Unfortunately, no one wanted to touch her. Sipping her wine, Dahl wondered if she really had lost it.

At the top of her game for years, she had transformed her skills in the kitchen into a multi-million-dollar business. Somewhere between the TV shows, renovating restaurants and books, she realized that she had become downright bored. Of course, she would never admit any of that out loud. Too many people depended on her for income, starting with her television show staff straight down to her agent. Dahl came to the stark realization that she didn't want to do it anymore.

A knock at the door snapped her out of her pity party. She pushed herself off the floor and grabbed her favorite blue jean shirt on her way past.

Having eaten nothing but take-out for two days straight, Dahl couldn't wait to go to paradise. She hadn't boiled even a pot of water since she'd left Bane's.

"Hold on," she called when the knock repeated.

Over her slip, she buttoned the shirt all the way to her breasts. Running through the top five places on her short list to visit, Dahl opened the door. Instead of the delivery driver bringing her sweet and sour chicken, wonton soup and egg rolls, her cousin greeted her.

"What?" She sighed. *Who do I have to kill for a fortune cookie?*

Grabbing a lock of her hair, she twisted it around her finger. Melanie opened her mouth but quickly shut it.

"Okay." Dahl began to shut the door.

"Wait." Her cousin slapped the thick wood with her palm. "I, uh, wanted to say I'm sorry."

"Cool." Since Dahl had no intention of assuaging her cousin's guilt, she made another attempt to close the door.

"And I shouldn't have brought up your fertility issues." Melanie spoke faster. "You were right. I've never really worked for anything and Trey is cheating on me."

Music to my ears. Dahl stopped herself from slamming the door in her cousin's face. In need of gossip and a good dose of other people's problems, she decided to listen a smidge longer.

"But it's not with Beth, my manager." She wiped a tear from her cheek. "She's gay. But, shit..."

"Really? Gay? I never would have guessed."

"Yeah, she amps up the whole flirting with men thing, but her parents are conservative Baptists, so she stays in the closet."

"Uh, isn't she thirty-five?"

"Yup, but they give her an allowance." Melanie shrugged.

Dahl took a swig from her wine, shocked that people that old received an allowance from mommy and daddy. "What's that crap you two tried to pull with the rapey quarterback at the auction?"

"We thought a date with our chef and Shawn would look good for the restaurant," Melanie said.

"Regardless of his shitty reputation?" Dahl pushed.

Her cousin at least had the good sense to look away. "Look… Bane outbid him. Can I come in or do you want all your neighbors to know my business?"

Dahl hadn't seen anyone besides the Uber Eats dude in days. "Fine, but if you pull any more of that stupid shit, I'm kicking you out."

She stepped away from the door and let her cousin enter.

"Wow, this place is nice," Mel said, looking around.

Dahl considered her cool bachelorette pad to be a fun spot. She hoped to get better-than-market price. "There's no way you're here because of Trey."

"Cheating on me is nothing new, but fucking over my money…" Melanie grabbed the bottle of wine off the table then wagged her finger in Dahl's direction. "I don't play with that shit." She took a huge swig. "Whatcha got to eat?"

Right on time, someone knocked on the door. Despite being stick thin, her cousin never turned down free grub. Dahl opened the door and paid the delivery man who was arriving with the Chinese food. With no other choice but to share, she took the bag and walked to her dining table to divvy up her order.

"Trey wants to be Bane so bad, but without all the hard work that comes with it." Melanie followed her to the living room and popped a squat in front of the table. Obviously pleased as a peacock, her cousin waited for Dahl to serve the food.

She passed her a plastic fork from the bag and a carton.

"He had no real talent for football," Melanie muttered over a mouthful of shrimp fried rice, "but he figured if Bane could do it, how hard could it be?"

The mooch reached for an egg roll and bit off a big chunk. Dahl tried to keep in mind that the mother of three was a little drunk on rage, but it still grossed her out. "If it wasn't for me, we wouldn't be able to afford our half of the restaurant."

"Hm-m… I thought Trey used his 401k from the software company?"

Melanie shook her head and grabbed a fortune cookie from the table. After ripping the plastic wrapper off, she broke the cookie in half. "He made that up to get Bane to think he had the capital, but truthfully, I performed filthy sex acts with a cash app on the web."

"No-o." Dahl reached for her wine glass.

Her cousin read her fortune with a frown then tossed it to the side. "Girl, I was one step away from the pole. 'Melanicious' was my name and I had an awesome Mardi Gras mask to hide my face."

"Why are you telling me this?" Dahl asked. She chuckled over her the rim of her glass. There was no way Melanie was offering up something this good for nothing in return.

"Because I'm going to need you to go through the restaurant financials. I'm not business orientated, but I think Trey is doing some fraud shit."

"Whoa!"

"And if he's stealing from me, then he's definitely stealing from Bane. Speaking of which… Where is the big guy?" Melanie stuffed the cookie into her mouth and crunched away on the bland-tasting treat. "I would think you'd be riding that di—"

Dahl held up a hand to stop her. "Apparently he no longer needs my help, so I've been dismissed."

As Melanie snorted, she made air quotes with her fingers. "'Help' is code for fucking, right?"

"Cooking for the kids," Dahl corrected her.

"Whatever." She swatted at the air dismissively. "That shit was payback for your divorce. He never got over it."

"Who told you that?"

"Please… He barely held it together after you left. I think your dad had to fly out and give him a pep talk. That's what Trey told me, anyway."

"But Pops was using a cane by then."

"Which means Bane was pretty bad off if a crippled man had to come mend his broken heart." Melanie searched for something on the table, ultimately landing on the third bottle of wine and opening it.

Diagnosed with Parkinson's soon after she and Bane had been married, her father had deteriorated at a rapid pace. Dahl hadn't known he'd kept in touch with Bane.

"He just wants to dump you before you get a chance to dump him again. Well, first…again."

"Melanie." She growled at the stupid loop her cousin had gotten stuck in.

"First" — Melanie sniffed — "with all those kids to take care of, Bane probably doesn't want to risk playing around with you. Or at least that's my guess." Her cousin opened her mouth and chugged the wine like a seasoned pro. Pretty sure the mooch would polish off her last merlot, Dahl made plans for a store run.

Chapter Eighteen

Wrangling all the kids together was always a monstrous task, but corralling them for a designated time had been an altogether different—and nearly impossible—animal. They had made it to the courthouse with barely ten minutes to spare.

"Uncle Bane"—Cady shook his hand—"I have to pee."

He groaned. It never failed. No matter how many times he asked before they left, it simply didn't matter.

"How long will this take? I have to shoot another makeup tutorial." Alana posed for a selfie with her phone.

"Do not post a court selfie," he warned her.

"Uncle Bane, if this ends early, can I go to the stadium? They're having a luncheon for the ball boys and—"

"We'll see." He cut the kid short, tamping down the urge to give him a hard 'no'.

"First you get that one dumb nanny who slept all day," Ester fussed. "Then you turn around and get an even stupider nanny who tries to burn your house down." She unlocked the side latches of the baby carrier that he had on his chest. "And if that wasn't bad enough, you chased off a world-renowned chef, who not only made delicious food but genuinely liked the kids." She took the sleeping baby and rocked him. "Bane Carter, you don't use the sense God gave you."

"Are you talking about my Dolly?" Cady asked. She turned her little face up. "I miss her."

"Ester," he hissed through clench teeth, "I really don't need this right now."

"No." The old lady twisted her thin lips into a grim frown. "What you need is a swift kick in the ass."

"Swear jar," Cady piped up.

"Nope, sweetie. I'm an elder. It's in the rules that Mama Ester is allowed to swear."

"What rules?" The little girl tugged at the back of her dress. Since she had to act ladylike when she wore it, Bane hoped she didn't snatch it off before the court hearing.

"The rules of the universe. Come on." Ester put out her hand for Cady but kept her glare on Bane. "Lucky for your stubborn behind, you have me. Don't mess it up this time. Alana and Jarin, go find us a seat in the courtroom. Cady, come with me."

"What the hell are you rambling about?" Bane asked, completely baffled. "Don't mess *what* up?"

She nodded her head to a spot over his shoulder before she walked away. Bane turned around to catch Dahl grabbing her purse off the security X-ray belt.

That warm, intense feeling he didn't trust squeezed his chest tight and wouldn't let up. The last two weeks had been hell without her. Bane hated the fact that he had not only relied on Dahl but craved her company. He'd tried to cut off that tap. The first time she'd broken his heart had been bad enough. A second time would simply destroy him.

Before his brain could stop the disloyal actions of his body, he walked down the long corridor and met her halfway.

"Let me guess... Ester?" Dahl graced him with a small smile. Bending dangerously close to her lips, he reached over and ripped the price tag off her sexy black suit.

"Dammit, Bane," she gasped, "I bought this specifically for court. When have you ever seen me wear adult clothes?"

"Color me shocked." He bit back a laugh at her expense. "It's not like you can't afford it."

Bane held out his hand, and Dahl snatched the tags out of his palm. "What? No 'I'm sorry'?"

"For what? I owed you one." Of course he should apologize, and she deserved it from the first time she'd left. Dahl tilted her head to the side, probably weighing all her options. "There's security on each floor. Whatever you're thinking, forget about it," he told her then smirked. "Besides, where did you park your white horse? I mean, you do seem to like saving me."

"If I'm not appreciated, Carter..." She took a step back, but he snagged her by the waist and pulled her into him.

"No one said you weren't appreciated," he whispered before he released her. "Thank you for coming."

"You can thank me later." Dahl slipped from his touch with a sexy chuckle and walked to their assigned courtroom. Rubbing his hand along the back of his head, he stared at her ass in that skintight skirt.

Stress was motivating Bane. He needed to work it off fairly quickly or it would squat inside of him. Either sex or the football field always worked best. Since he'd opened his eyes that morning, he'd been nervous about court. For the first time that day, he immediately felt things had looked up. Bane opened the door.

"After you, sweetheart." They stepped into the courtroom.

Since Devon had made an airtight will, Bane didn't think they would be there long.

"Carter vs. Alvarez," the court administrator called. He joined his huge squad and ushered them to the defendants' table in front of the judge.

Several seconds later, his lawyer joined them. "This is a preliminary hearing for custody of the Carter children. Your Honor, my client has sole custody of the four children, and he is the closest living relative who resides in the United States. This is where the children's parents wished for them to be raised."

Opposing counsel spoke. "My client is a brother to Isabella Carter, formerly known as Alvarez, and he lives in the US with his wife and two children. Carlos Alvarez is petitioning the courts for custody. He believes there's another will that hasn't been located as of yet."

Bane's lawyer replied, "Unless he can produce this phantom will, Judge, I will have to ask the court to toss out this frivolous petition."

"Unlike Mr. Carter, my client has a stable home life," opposing counsel said.

As Bane stared the man down, Dahl whispered something to his lawyer. "My client has a good school district, professional help with the kids and a fiancée."

"Wha—" Bane began to object.

Dahl elbowed him in the side. "Go with it," she muttered under her breath.

The judge peered over the top of her reading glasses at them. "For how long?"

"A few months," she lied with ease.

"Don't I know you from somewhere?"

"Maybe The Culinary Channel."

The judged nodded.

"Uh, excuse me, Your Honor. Mr. Carter's dating life shouldn't have any bearing on this proceeding. My client has been in a successful marriage for over fifteen years."

"His client isn't here, Judge," Bane's lawyer coughed out. "And besides, he's the one who brought up the question of a stable home life."

"How long have you two known each other?" the judge asked Dahl.

Well aware where this line of questioning could lead, Bane groaned to himself.

"Since college. We were married roughly eighteen years ago," Dahl offered up sweetly.

"And you want another go at it?" The judge took off her glasses with a wicked twinkle in her eye. She was either a delightful instigator or a hard, nosey litigator. Bane didn't know which way to lean on this one. "Well, what's the hold up? Neither one of you are getting any younger."

Definitely an instigator, he decided.

"Excuse me?" Dahl asked.

"The upside is that both of you are well established, but quite frankly, time is ticking." The judge tapped the face of her watch.

Dahl opened her mouth but quickly snapped it shut.

But the judge was obviously not going to let it go. "We can do it now. I mean, you two did it once before, so…"

"Uh, we don't have a license," Dahl mumbled. "And maybe I want a big wedding." She tapped her nail nervously against the tabletop. "We had a small one last time, so—"

"That works for me," Bane interjected, honestly loving every minute of this. At any time he could have saved her, but she deserved to sweat.

"Great, then that's settled. We'll adjourn for two weeks then revisit this case. Perhaps the couple will have a date set by then." The judge glanced down at the papers and spouted off instructions to her clerk of the court.

"Hold on," Dahl squeaked.

"Judge, what about my client's petition for custody?" opposing counsel interrupted.

"An updated and authenticated will has to be submitted to the court before I can even consider taking this petition seriously."

"Mr. Carter has an open case pending with DCFS." The lawyer pouted. He was actually whining worse than Alana did.

"I read the preliminaries, and it appears to be a nothing burger." Without looking up, the judge quickly flipped through the file in front of her.

"Pardon me, but this is child neglect we're talking—"

"We'll reconvene in two weeks." The judge slammed her gavel on the block with a slight chuckle.

"What just happened?" Dahl asked.

"You can always chase her down and tell her the truth."

"Isn't that like perjury or something?" Dahl frowned.

Jarin tugged on the sleeve of his suit jacket. "Does this mean I can go to the stadium, Uncle Bane?"

"I've heard of unorthodox judges," opposing counsel complained on his way out of the door, "but this is ridiculous."

Bane pulled the dazed Dahl into his chest. "Go with it," he whispered in her ear before he led a trail of kisses to her lips.

* * * *

The brash sounds of bells and cartoons playing in the background did nothing for her nerves. Mildly shocked, she sat across the booth from Bane in the kid-friendly restaurant, wide eyed and confused.

"Are you two going to have a real wedding — or at least a reception?" Alana leaned in front of the table with her phone to pose for a group photo.

Everyone ignored her.

"Is it me or is this place more obnoxious in person than it is on TV?" Bane asked, seeming completely unfazed. Even a twitch of nerves would have assured her that she wasn't crazy.

As she watched him feed the baby his bottle, Dahl itched to swipe that grin off his face.

"Why didn't Jarin have to come? Ester could have taken me with her," Alana complained.

Apparently lying to a judge qualified as one sin too many for Ester. She had commandeered Bane's truck and taken off. Dahl arched an eyebrow in his direction over Cady's head. The kid was sitting on her lap and coloring on the kids' menu.

"The stadium is on the way to her church," he told Alana then turned to Dahl. "You're awfully quiet over there." He shot her a lopsided grin. *She's truly irresistible.*

Dahl met his gaze across the table. "Nope, just plotting." She winked in return.

"What about a ring? Doesn't she get a ring, Uncle Bane?" the teen asked.

"She got a ring the first time," he groused.

"That doesn't count." Alana laughed then resumed making stupid faces into her phone.

New filters, Dahl figured. Nothing ever kept the teenager's attention this long.

"It does when she never gave it back," he said with a pointed stare.

"I beg your pardon, but I gave it to Trey to give to you."

Bane shifted the baby to his shoulder to pat him on the back. "Has Trey ever done the right thing?"

"Well, shit."

"Swear jar!" Cady hollered.

"If she sticks around for a year, she'll get another one," Bane told them.

"Wow, a whole year, you say?" she mimicked him.

"Consider it a down payment." Bane pointed at her. "We can easily go back and tell that nice judge you made it all up."

Tempted to toss a crayon at his pretty mug, Dahl sighed. "We have Cady's birthday party then Jarin's gamer convention. If I'm in jail, it will put a damper on the next few weeks."

"No-o," Alana cried. She took her attention off the phone long enough to whine, "It's not fair." The teen's whole face scrunched down into a wicked sneer. "Why do we all have to go?"

"When it's your turn to torture Jarin, remember this exact moment."

"Sorry, Dahl, but I have to agree with Alana. There's no way—"

"You either." She squinted her eyes in Bane's direction, daring him to challenge her on this one. "We're all stuck." She made a wide circle around the table. "All. Now deal."

Thankfully, the waiter picked the perfect time to bring the food. "I hear congratulations are in order," the pimply face teen bellowed at the top of his lungs as a group of his co-workers surrounded them.

"One peep out of any of you and I will lose my shit," she threatened the squad of hormonal teenagers.

"Swear jar," Cady screamed over the ridiculously loud noises that poked at Dahl's brain. Bane's deep laughter and quiet murmurs of disappointment from the staff worked their way over the noise.

Dahl needed a drink.

Chapter Nineteen

The remodeled kitchen showed no signs of a fire and had been outfitted with all the latest gadgets and appliances. Dahl wanted to pitch a tent and live there forever. Since the fresh coat of paint still had to dry before they could move back in, she'd ended up sneaking over to bake during the middle of the night. She wore a long slip nightie, but even with the doors and windows open, it was ridiculously hot. Fully understanding that if she turned on the air it would be the equivalent of blowing money out of the windows, Dahl was still tempted to do it.

Low on time, she was forced to knock the majority of the birthday menu out before tomorrow afternoon. Dahl focused on the whir from the twirling mixer. She whipped the cake batter into shape and ran off the rest of the planned treats in her head.

"One more day, Dahl, then we can move back. The paint has to dry." The baritone of his deep voice tickled her ear. Bane wrapped his arms around her, forcing her to lean back into his hard, naked chest.

"But if I don't do this now, then no cake." He rubbed his crotch against her ass. "Where was all this energy a few weeks ago?"

Bane moved her hair off her shoulders and kissed her neck.

"Honey, I love fucking you, but I'm not looking to die doing it." Dahl didn't want to laugh at Bane, but she couldn't help it. "Over a certain age, air conditioning becomes a necessity."

She turned to face him, knocking into a wall of muscle. "We could have gone somewhere else."

"Like where…? The car? Refer back to my last statement."

"Nobody wants to hear that," she warned him.

With a devilish glint in his eye, Bane leaned down and landed small pecks to her lips. If she didn't have a million things to do, she would climb onto the counter and screw him silly. He nibbled on her top lip, then gently sought out her tongue.

"Don't bother me, I'm working," she murmured against his warm mouth. The slut that lived inside her head demanded she spread her legs for him.

"Is that right?" Bane ran his hand underneath her slip. "We've got to make up properly or that lady judge will come and cart you off to jail."

"Me? I lied for *you*," she said.

He moved her slip up her thigh and flicked her nub with his thumb. "Nobody asked you to." Bane claimed her mouth with a moan. "But aren't you lucky that I didn't tell the truth and have you carted off to the slammer? Thank God I don't have to pretend with you." Bane ran his hand gently through her pussy lips.

"Oh, is that what you think you got out of this deal, familiar pus—?"

A loud crash rumbled deep within the house. It forced Bane to release her. "Are all the kids in the cottage?" he asked.

Startled, she nodded.

"Stay here." He took off down the hall toward his office.

Maybe one of the workmen had left his tools on the edge of his bookcase or desk. Dahl tentatively stepped around the island and walked closer to the foyer to listen.

"Hey!" Bane roared. Dahl heard hard feet against wood thundering down the hall. "Call the police!" he shouted to her.

"Bane, what's going on?"

"Stay here!" He sprinted out of the patio doors.

Rage pumped through his veins as he was running in search of the man he had caught climbing out of his office window. He swiveled his head from left to right. *A gated community... I live in a freaking gated community.* The HOA fees alone should have ensured his family's safety, but *no!* Dead in the middle of the night, he was searching for someone he could legally pound into the ground.

A fast-moving blur ducked into the shrubs nearest the guest house. It led to a path that circled the neighbor's pool and ended at the guard's entrance. Bane cut a diagonal swath across the grass and leaped onto the intruder's back. He managed to knock him to the ground, but the flexible little turd wiggled loose.

When Bane made a grab for his leg, a burst of pain exploded near his eye. Pure anger fueled his downward punch. He hoped he'd connected with the asshole's crotch.

"Arghh," the dude groaned. At least he had hurt the idiot. The intruder worked out of his grip. Bane tried to get up but rocked back on his feet. Confused by the blood that dripped into his eye, he nearly got hit on the other side of his head but blocked the hard object with his forearm. Fast as hell, the little shit swung at him again, but jerked backward with a scream.

With the gun trained on the burglar, who was crab-walking backward, Dahl stalked past him. Before she could fire off another round, Bane yanked her by the waist and forced her arm to the ground, even though that let the perpetrator escape into the trees.

"Shit, Bane. I almost had him." Lights from the surrounding houses flipped on.

Holding her tight in a bear hug, his heart slamming into his chest wall, he fought back the mounting fear. "That's the problem," Bane said.

* * * *

Police came in and out of the house, collecting evidence. Dahl continued to work in the kitchen, the same one she had been asked to stay out of until the next day.

As far as she could tell, the paint had dried well enough. If the warnings from a construction foreman hadn't scared her off, why would the unexpected appearance of a cat burglar?

"Let me see if I have this right," the female cop asked her. "The house was off limits and you took it upon yourself to bake?" Officer Miller's snooty tone wasn't lost on Dahl.

"Tomorrow is Cady's fifth birthday party." While Dahl mixed the batter, she ran down her to-do list in her head.

"And that was worth sneaking over to an empty house for?"

Dahl cast her a withering glance. She was too far behind to deal with this woman.

"By Mr. Carter's and your own admission," Officer Miller spoke slowly, probably deciding Dahl was an idiot, "there was a suspicious fire at the house a few weeks ago. Didn't you think to err on the side of caution?"

Tired of the senseless third degree, she reined in any smart retort. "It seems more dangerous to throw a kid's party with no treats than worry about paint. Besides" — she waved off the cop's concerns — "the foreman promised this would be done days ago."

"Grocery store cupcakes aren't good enough for you?" The cop rolled her eyes and blew out a huge breath. "Okay, you didn't get a real good look at the guy, but you place him around five-foot-ten to six feet tall with olive skin. Perhaps early-to-mid-twenties, correct?"

"Yup, you got it." She put down the bowl and loaded the paper cups into the pan. The to-go bags were next, and she still needed to tackle the big cake. Dahl would knock out the prep for the mini pizza, hot dogs and sliders last.

"What do you think this person wanted?"

"They went through all my personal information," Bane said. He'd stepped into the kitchen from the patio door. After he had initially spoken to the cops, he'd gone to the guest house to check on the kids for the second time. "I don't have much work stuff at the house, but the drawer with all the kids' information was broken."

"Information such as?" Officer Miller seemed downright friendly when she spoke to Bane.

"Medical information, school records and a copy of their parents' will… Some of those files are missing."

The woman's hardened expression seemed to soften at the mention of the kids' parents. "Okay, I'll pass all this information on to the officers working your arson case. Someone may have to follow up with you tomorrow. I think it's admirable what you're doing for those poor kids."

"Thank you, Officer…"

"Miller." She quickly offered Bane a toothy smile. "Abigail Miller. My friends call me Abby."

It was Dahl's turn to roll her eyes at the ridiculous groupie with a badge.

"Okay. Well, thank you…Officer Miller."

As Bane escorted her to the front door, Dahl opened the oven and grabbed the cookies from the rack. Seriously behind, she went into stealth mode and flipped on her automatic pilot switch. Deeply immersed in her thoughts, she didn't even hear Bane come back to the kitchen.

"Why would you have a gun in the house? I hate guns, and you above anyone else know that," Bane said to her.

"Good news… They confiscated it for evidence. Problem solved."

"What if — ?"

"He'd gotten the best of you and knocked you unconscious — or worse?" she threw back at him.

After spending the last hour entertaining Officer Mac-Thotty, Dahl didn't have the energy for this fight.

She needed to move fast if the kids wanted to eat delicious treats in a few hours. Bane's little heart-to-heart was not only unnecessary but unwelcome.

"That's not what happened," he growled.

"Could have been. Then what?"

"Dahl…"

"Look…" She picked up the bag of kisses to decorate the top of the cookies. "Your schedule is all over the place and that's putting it mildly." When he opened his mouth, she tilted her head to the side and leveled him with her best glare. Probably thinking better of it, he allowed her to continue. "Not to mention that the security guards at the front gate aren't the most astute crime fighters, as this break-in has certainly proven. With that said, I'm sorry that I wasn't more upfront about the gun, but I don't regret having it."

Rubbing his hand over his face, he groaned. Bane turned away and walked out of the patio door, most likely figuring he wouldn't win this round.

Chapter Twenty

The tiny gremlins were everywhere. Dressed as various fairytale characters, fifty or more little kids had taken over his property. With how tired he was after the previous night's excitement, Bane didn't know how much more of the incessant running, screaming and shooting pain in his head he could deal with.

"What's the end time on this party?" he asked. After the police had taken their statement last night, Dahl had spent the rest of the night in the kitchen. Considering they'd had very little rest, he should probably cut her some slack, but subtlety wasn't his strong suit, so he'd avoided talking to her up to this point.

"Hm-m, no more silent treatment," she muttered. While Dahl loaded the tray with more kiddie cupcakes, Bane picked through a bowl of candy.

"It was better than me hollering at you."

She reached across and slid the candy bowl away from him.

"And why would you do that?" She gave him a wan smile. He knew better than to keep this up. Smarter with no sleep than most people were awake, she slid her tight little body next to him. Did he believe Dahl wanted to make out in front of a house full of children? Of course not. She simply wanted to place herself into verbal punching distance to deliver a body blow.

"Kids plus guns is a bad combination," he stated the obvious. He kept his gaze locked with hers.

"Generally, yes, but that gun saved you from getting your head bashed in, so..." She traced her finger along the edge of the Band-Aid on his head. The cops had recommended stitches, but one more scar in his collection made little difference.

"Dahl, honey, you know why I don't want a gun in the house," he said in a hushed tone.

As far as he was concerned, his reactions to thunderstorms and guns were understandable. However, he had no power over nature. He could only do something about the latter. He touched the side of her face, and she moved her head against his hand.

"Yes, Bane, I do, and it was an unfortunate childhood trauma that I wish had never happened to you. But that doesn't negate the fact that I saved your ass last night."

Just as he was ready to belabor the point about the textbook meaning of trauma, several cartoon characters surrounded them. "Dolly, are the cupcakes ready?" Cady asked.

"Yes, sweetie. Go outside. Your uncle will bring them out." The horde of kids and their cacophony of colors ran out of the house. Dahl reached for the tray of cupcakes and handed them over. "Here... Make yourself useful."

Opening his mouth to convey where these cupcakes could actually go, he watched as Dahl raised her eyebrow. Thinking better of it, he abruptly crossed the kitchen and walked out of the patio doors. Mobbed by tiny Disney and Pixar characters, he set the tray down.

Similar to a clan of hyenas with their kill, the group of little ones destroyed the platter of pastries in seconds.

"This food, man…" Warner snagged a tiny dessert out of the hands of one of the crumb snatchers. "I've got to tell you." He bit into the small pastry with groan. "Snickers? You've got to introduce me to the cook."

"Don't worry. There's another tray coming," he announced to the group. Woody the cowboy nodded sadly and wandered toward the men on stilts. "Why the hell are you here?" Bane asked him.

The agent nodded toward a family nearby. "Potential clients. I've got to show them how much I respect the family unit."

"Does he even play football?"

Warner reached for one of the Dixie cups of punch on the snack table. "In his country, that's what it's called."

"Why did you bring a soccer player to my house?"

Warner tried to hide his slick smile behind the mini cupcake pastry. "A few of my clients can talk me up to the kid. He's one of the top players overseas."

Alana brought another tray of treats out. The kids quickly mobbed her on sight.

The agent snatched another dessert off the tray before Alana could put them down on the table. "Have you seen some of these kids? I would give them less than five minutes before they mugged the Good Humor man with a toy gun. You can't keep shooting them up with sugar and think they won't go out looking for their next fix. Did that chef from the restaurant make these?"

"Yeah. I bribed her with a whole lot of shit." Bane nodded toward the food table. "She's Tinkerbell over there."

As Warner choked on white frosting, Dahl set up an oasis of mini hot dogs, pizza and sliders. The agent beat his chest and turned in her direction. He cleared his throat and shoved the rest of the pastry into his mouth. "That's not Tinkerbell." Luminous wings were harnessed to the back of Dahl's glittery green fairy costume. "She's the Absinthe fairy."

Bane grunted. "I'll take your word for it."

"Which makes her fun. Too bad I didn't meet her first."

"Yeah, well, she's also wife number one. You would have had to get a twenty-year jump on me."

The asshole agent graced him with a big, country-boy howl. "She's the one who didn't want to be stuck with a vegetable, huh?"

"Oversimplifying." At some point he must have told Warner about Dahl, probably in a drunken moment. "Her father was diagnosed with Parkinson's and I was on my third concussion, but I lied and told the league it was numero uno. She gave me an ultimatum, and I—"

"May I?" The sports agent held up his hand with a chuckle. "You called her bluff and stepped back onto the field without a care in the world."

"It sounds like you've picked a side."

"Considering you were over the protocol limit, it's pretty much hers. 'Until death do us part' has its limits, Romeo," Warner admitted. "I'm surprised she'd be anywhere in the vicinity of someone as stubborn as you."

"Says the man who has a revolving door to his bedroom."

"Hey, what you see is what you get. At least I'm honest. And on that note…" He waved at his potential client. "I have to go to my next family fun event and win over this dude. You should probably go save your hot fairy chef from the cop."

Bane scanned the yard. Dahl wasn't by the food table anymore. He found his tawdry wet dream at the edge of the driveway with a dude in a suit. After they shook hands, she escorted him to the side door of Bane's office.

"How do you know he's a cop?"

"I'm a sports agent. I can spot them a mile away." Warner slapped his hand against Bane's and hit him with a half hug. "Catch me later. We need to talk."

"I thought that's what we were doing?" He headed toward the patio to see what the hell the cop wanted.

"Big, bad adult crap, I'm afraid," Warner called after him. "Too many ears."

Dodging more than his fair share of keyed-up kids, Bane made his way to the house.

Chapter Twenty-One

Dahl led the officer into Bane's den. "Do you have children, Officer Garcia?"

"Two boys and a girl." She grabbed the party platter of cookies off his desk. The cop surveyed the treats before he made a grab for the double chocolate chunks. "Thanks." He tipped the huge cookie at her and took a bite. "Mm-m, these are good."

What the shit? She was an award-winning chef. *What the hell did he think it would taste like? Cardboard?* Dahl struggled to keep her expression pleasant. "Please take a couple of gift bags when you leave."

"No, I couldn't."

"We have more than enough. Besides, it might make up for you working on a Saturday afternoon."

He provided her with a slight nod. Dahl still wasn't sure if he would take the bags or not as he took a seat on the couch.

"So what can I do for you?" Dahl leaned against Bane's huge wood desk. Beyond tired, she counted the minutes until the party would be over

163

"A couple of follow-up questions, then I'll be out of your hair." He took a small notepad and pen from inside of his suit jacket. "Congratulations on your engagement, by the way."

Confused at how he knew, since Dahl didn't have a ring, she merely nodded in acceptance. Thankfully, Bane picked that moment to appear.

"Are you and Mr. Carter getting married to ensure the custody of the children?"

"No," Bane answered. He stood in the doorway of the office. "I got it right the first time. It just took her a couple of decades to catch up."

The officer struggled to stand, but Bane waved him down and offered his hand to shake.

"Lou Garcia," he introduced himself. "This morning I caught the report on that break-in last night, and after your fire a few weeks ago, I decided to follow up. I didn't mean to intrude on your party."

"Not a problem. We can use a break from the chaos."

Bane took a spot next to Dahl. "What does our pending marriage have to do with the break-in yesterday?"

"Well, let's start at the beginning. What's the custody case about?"

"My brother and his wife died, and her family is contesting the will," Bane told him.

Garcia flipped through the notes in his tiny pad. "They died in a car accident in Brazil, correct?"

"Yes."

"From what I've been able to dig up, your brother purchased a farm there for his in-laws."

"Huh?" Dahl glanced over at Bane. Other than the vein that bulged on his neck, he appeared relaxed.

"Financially, his wife's family was having a hard time. Your brother was sending them funds to keep them afloat. It looks like he bought the farm to relieve some of their burdens."

Bane blew out a breath. "What type of farm?"

"Coffee beans — and it wasn't doing well. I called the local police down there. Either the family was being extorted or they were seriously bad with money."

"And the accident?"

"Flat tire at night. With little to no visibility, a passing truck careened into them."

"Foul play?" Dahl asked.

"Honestly, I thought the same thing." Garcia closed his notebook. "But no, it was an accident."

"How does any of this relate to the break-in?" Bane's energy seemed to change drastically toward the dark end of the spectrum.

"The custody case."

"Shit," he hissed. "They think I'll pay them off to get the kids back if they win custody?"

"That's my guess," the officer told them. "Whoever broke in last night was probably looking for the will."

"Didn't they get a copy?"

"Not if they weren't in it. Her family has probably never seen the will's contents. In some way, they probably thought it would help them with the custody case if they knew what was in it — not to mention that I believe they paid off that deranged nanny to set your house on fire."

Pinching the bridge of his nose, Bane took a deep breath.

"There's not a whole lot I can do about the investigation of your brother." Officer Garcia stood up. "You'll have to contact the Rio police for that." He handed Bane a card and pointed at the cookie tray. "Do you mind? These are really good."

Well, duh... Dahl plastered that lukewarm smile back on her face as Bane's phone went off. He reached into his back pocket.

"If I hear anything I'll let you know."

She walked Officer Garcia to the side door to see him out.

"Oh, come on!" he groaned. Bane flipped his cell around for her to see.

"Shit." Dahl danced around in a frenzy. *Where the hell did I leave my keys? Crap... Or my phone, for that matter.* She hadn't seen it in hours. "Birthday cake! Get these off of me," she screamed, pointing at her wings. "We'll just move the 'Happy Birthday' song up, then I can go—"

"Oh hell no, Dahl! You're not leaving." He pushed his face in front of hers. "Do you understand me?"

"Either you deal with adults that haven't gotten paid in weeks or a dozen five-year-olds. Pick your poison."

"Does that shit work with other people?" he asked. She turned away from him to unfasten her wings. "More than fifty gremlins are loose in my house, all thanks to you."

"Unhook me!" she demanded.

Bane blew out a breath that heated the back of her neck. "If I have to choose between those kids and Trey"—he yanked her harness tight to make a point, and she chuckled at his childish antics—"that restaurant can burn to the ground for all I care."

"And if we leave Melanie and Trey in charge of it for one minute longer, it will." Free of the cumbersome wings, Dahl turned around and sweetly kissed him on the lips. "Now suck it up, buttercup. We've got a song to sing."

* * * *

Angry energy attacked her from all sides. Dahl stood in front of the restaurant crew with a huge marinara stain on the front of her stupid fairy costume and she cleared her throat. A room full of pissed-off First Down employees glared at her. "Thank you guys for your patience," she began.

A Disney character delivering the apology had to lessen the blow of not getting paid a little, *right?* As an okay public speaker, she not only felt slightly nervous but also super embarrassed to boot. "If you don't want to stay on with First Down while they make changes in management, I'll understand. Here are your paychecks for the last two pay periods, and once again, please accept my heartfelt apology."

After they'd sung *Happy Birthday* and cut Cady's cake, Dahl had left Bane to wrap up the party. She'd hightailed it over to the restaurant to arrive minutes prior to a full-fledged mutiny. Melanie's stupid ass had barricaded herself in the manager's office. Once Dahl had promised her cousin that no one would beat her senseless, she'd unlocked the door.

It took her a while, but Dahl had finally managed to piece together the damage. Not the most cunning criminal mastermind, Trey had taken off with a whole lot of money. Since Bane had to sign off on different accounts, he hadn't stolen all of it. To pay off the staff, she'd had to call in a couple of favors. Thankfully, most of their vendors had agreed to late payments.

"Sorry," Melanie mumbled to each staff member who stood in line to collect their check. Leaving her cousin to finish the grunt work, Dahl hit the shower in the manager's office. She couldn't take the fairy costume — not one more second.

Why Trey needed to wash his ass here and not at home, Dahl didn't want to wager a guess. She stepped into his tacky office and headed straight to the bathroom. Pretty sure she had a few more hours of bills to go over, she didn't want to do it with the aroma of deep-dish pizza in her pores.

Twisting the shower knob, Dahl squirted his Old Spice shower gel into her hand and scrubbed birthday party sweat and restaurant hate off her skin. A quick rinse cycle would help her get a second wind.

She twisted the water knob off and grabbed the towel on the rack. Sniffing it first, she prayed it was safe. After she got home, another shower would be in order. Dahl needed to rid herself of the weird shower ick from the first one. Ready to tackle a few more invoices, she opened the door. The last thing she expected to find was her sexy ex-husband Bane sitting behind Trey's desk, reading the open file.

"Please tell me this fool didn't just steal from me," he seethed. Dahl had left his cousin's financial statement on the desk. Anyone with a smidge of sense could figure out Trey's crappy breadcrumb trail.

"Why, Bane Carter, I thought you wanted this place to burn to the ground." Poking the bear probably wouldn't help.

"Lord knows I enjoy your 'bygones be bygones' spirit, but the next time I see Trey, trust and believe that I'm fucking him up on sight."

"Get in line. Melanie thinks he took off with his favorite stripper from the Pink Monkey."

"Seriously?"

As she crossed the room, Dahl pulled the rubber band out of her hair. She shook her curls free to fall around her shoulders. Bane pushed his chair back and placed his big hands on her waist to help her onto the desk. "Since you're the expert, I will defer to your wisdom. Should gasoline and a lighter be put to this place?"

"Good news." Dahl spread her legs for him. "Melanie is going to sell me their half."

"And you think that's enough to save this mess of a restaurant?" As he leaned back in the chair, Bane lowered his gaze to her crotch.

"It's a start." Craving some relief, she opened her legs a little wider. The day had been nothing better than a dumpster fire.

He placed his hand on her knee and slowly moved his way up her leg. "Did it bother you when the cop insinuated we were only together for the kids?"

"Uh...no." Caught off guard, she leaned back. "I mean, it's a just a joke, right?"

"According to who?" Bane's warm eyes locked with hers, and his gaze never wavered.

"Well, you and the judge." Dahl licked her lips and wondered, *When the hell did my mouth become so dry?*

"To be clear"—he moved his hand under her towel—"watching the judge back you into a corner was funny, but once we go back to court, you can tell her we want to wait or..."

"Or?" Her chest tightened at his words.

"Tell her we want to get married." As his huge finger touched her clit, she exhaled. Bane kept his eyes on hers and circled his thumb on her nub. Grabbing the sides of her thighs, he pulled her toward him. Dahl's ass dangled off the edge of the desk. "The ball is in your court."

Infuriating at the wrong times, the big, sexy man had these moments of pure sweetness that rocked her world.

"I've never *not* loved you, Dahl." With a hint of a smile, he held her gaze.

Determined not to melt into a puddle of mush, she glanced away from his intense stare. "How would I know? You don't talk much."

"Shower and a grower, just not a talker." He reached up and flicked the knot of her towel between his fingers. Instantly exposed, she tipped her head back up to face him. "Forewarning… I'm too old to play games. Either you're in or you're out."

Bane lowered his head and blew on her exposed clit then pecked her swollen nub.

"Oh!"

As he darted his tongue in and out of her opening, Dahl grew weak from the intensity. She dropped her head back and moaned. Weeks had passed by without this type of attention. Between the fire, court and her birthday party duties, Dahl needed this. Grabbing the back of his head, she ground her pussy against his mouth. Waves of pleasure shook her core as Dahl moved her hips to the rhythm of his tongue.

Propping her foot against the back of his chair, she increased the friction. "Fuck," she groaned.

Bane sucked her clit hard. She didn't have to worry about inching toward the edge of the cliff. Dahl pitched all the way off. Still in the throes of a major orgasm, she watched as Bane stood up and fumbled with his pants.

Once he pushed them past his hips, he shoved his cock into her dripping pussy. Dahl had to hold on to the desk to take the ferocity of his thrusts. He pumped harder and faster inside her. Clearly holding nothing back, he slammed into her over and over.

Bane drew his hand down her chest before he palmed her breast. Capturing her nipple between his fingers, he rolled the bud.

Dahl screamed, without a care who was left in the restaurant.

"This pussy…" He sighed. "So good." Dahl pushed herself up to attack his mouth. "Baby, fuck," he muttered between nips to his skin and bites against his lips and tongue. Dahl matched his strokes, allowing his cock to fill her.

Overwhelming tingles started in her pussy and spread throughout her body. She thrust against him and hit her second orgasm in record time. While she clutched him tight within her walls, his cock pulsed inside her.

Chapter Twenty-Two

A stadium full of serious gamers took over the McCormick Center. Dahl was amazed at the level of professionalism that went into Jarin's favorite pastime. At the ripe old age of thirteen, the kid had placed in the first round. Although she was elated for his small victory, Dahl sincerely hoped he didn't make it to the finals. Their team spirit had hit a wall, not to mention that she honestly couldn't take a minute more of this nonstop techno crap.

On their way to the next round, they walked through the hallway. So far, the competition was made up of mostly young boys and not very many girls.

"Dolly, I'm hungry," Cady whined.

"Yeah, when can we go?" Alana asked from where she trailed behind their small unit, engrossed in her phone.

"Oh my ghad!" a group of tweens screamed. Dahl whipped around but had no idea who had gained their undivided attention. "Make Me Alana!" they cried her YouTube channel name.

"Dahl…" Alana drew close, tugging on the bottom of her tank top.

"We watch all your videos," one of the crazed kids screamed.

"Wing eyeliner, spider lashes!" another said, who seemed more unhinged than the last.

"And matte lipstick, awwk!"

Dahl squealed in surprise at their jacked-up energy.

"Wow, you watch my show?" Alana asked.

"We have sleepovers and practice all your techniques. Can we take a selfie?" They all hugged in close.

Dahl didn't want to interrupt their weird stalker moment, but if they wanted to get good seats inside for the next round, they needed to get a move on. She held up her finger at Bane, who was waiting for them down the hall.

While the girls huddled close to take selfies, Cady shook her hand. She glanced down at the sleepy kid. "Dolly, this is weird."

"Tell me about it," she muttered.

Once they got all the giggly crap out of the way, Alana practically floated over to them. "That was so-o cool," she said.

"Check it out, Alana fans. Maybe we can monetize your channel," Dahl suggested.

"Like, get money for it?"

"Why not? You're an influencer now and we need all the money we can get."

"What?" Alana's pretty face switched to confused uncomfortably fast.

"Kidding." She chuckled. Last night after her second session of that taboo ex-sex, Bane had explained the state of the Mavericks. Add all her own failing endeavors to the mix and they were officially a mess.

As they started back down the hall, a skinny, older version of Bane's brother walked out of the game room.

"Granddaddy!" Alana hollered and ran toward him, with Cady hot on her heels.

Dahl resisted the urge to ease away in the opposite direction. Bane hated surprises, and his father, James Carter, being there was a huge one.

* * * *

After grabbing the two smoothies from the cashier, Bane headed to the table where his father was waiting for him. They weren't close. There was too much history in the way. However, he mentally thanked the man. The loud noises and crazy colors from the video games were driving him crazy, and he needed a break.

"Back with Dahl, huh?" James Carter asked him. With wide-set eyes and a face longer than his, his brother Devon had resembled his dad. Bane looked more like his mom. Bushy eyebrows and high cheekbones aside, he could probably pass for the man's son from a distance.

He handed over his drink. "She didn't call you?"

"No, Jarin told me. We text all the time."

"When the hell did you learn how to do that?" Bane hadn't realized that his dad had cultivated a relationship with his grandchildren.

Offering up a low chuckle, he nodded. "The kids taught me a while back. I'm not *that* technologically ignorant."

Bane drank the bitter green smoothie and frowned. *I should have added pineapple.* "Did you know about the farm?"

Dad shuffled his sneaker-covered feet around. *Is he nervous?* Bane couldn't be sure.

"Yeah. I told Devon it was a bad idea." His brother had had a better relationship with their dad than he did. Bane didn't want to call him an absentee father or anything, but 'emotionally unavailable' described him better. "Isabella's family was bleeding them dry. He thought the farm would..." Dad swatted his words away with his hand. "Your brother had too much heart."

Bane snorted. "Guess who he didn't get that from?"

"What do they call it nowadays...single dad? Hey, I did the best I could."

"Did you?"

They grew quiet, which made it awkward. In a minute, uncomfortable would knock on the door, inevitably forcing them further apart. Dad turned his head away and coughed. "There's no instruction manual on how to raise two kids by yourself."

"Pretty sure making an eleven-year-old play keep-away with a gun isn't in the prologue."

"Still having headaches during storms?" he muttered.

Bane nodded. Migraines and thunderstorms went hand in hand.

"Maybe you should talk to someone about that."

"Yeah, I am." He stared pointedly at his father. *Do I want to have this conversation?* Nope, but four kids were depending on him to work it out.

"She insisted on protection—and when she wasn't manic..." Dad rubbed his face and sighed.

Since his mom's bad days had outnumbered her good, Bane rarely remembered any part of his childhood that hadn't been riddled with chaos. After bouncing from one military post to another, his dad had thought it made sense for them to stay in the States. That way his mom could get better health care.

"Look… She would never willingly hurt you kids."

"What about herself?"

"Maybe I didn't want to see it." Taking the baseball cap off his head, his dad ran a hand over his bald spot.

Rainy days had amped his mom's anxiety, but thunderstorms had thrown her into a frenzy. Bane had been forced to create a routine. If she had an episode, he'd move the gun to another location then get Devon out of the house. Once the storm let up, he would wait another hour before returning back home.

"We looked for her for what seemed like forever, but…" Bane tuned his father out. It was always the same. The old man never deviated from the script. They hadn't found her then and never would. Dad had always hoped she'd merely run away, but Bane knew better.

That day, Devon had stayed home from school. At the first few drops of rain, Bane had ditched his homeroom and run the two blocks home. Unfortunately, she had already found the gun. Outside, he could hear her ranting and raving. Instead of confronting her, he'd gone to the bedroom window and snuck Devon out of the house. At eleven years old, he hadn't known what to do. His options had been limited. Regret for not calling the police still haunted him. After that day, Bane had never seen his mom again.

"You shouldn't blame yourself," his dad finished.

"Maybe I did at first, but then I started blaming you," Bane told him matter-of-factly. Three days later a neighbor had contacted his aunt. She'd taken the boys in until his dad could make it back to the States. Oddly enough, without his bipolar mom around, life had gotten harder, not easier. "Now, I don't know."

Since his dad had worked all the time, Bane had taken care of Devon. Football had become the one thing he'd done for himself. The game had helped him work out all the hate and anger instead of bottling it up.

"Seeing Devon's kids and how helpless they are, well..." Dad sighed. He put his hat back on and placed his hands on his smoothie cup. He was uncharacteristically fidgety, and Bane wondered what was up with the old man. "I'm...uh, sorry. You were just a child and you shouldn't have been put in that position."

There's a first time for everything. His father had never offered him an apology. Bane opened his mouth to tell him as much, but their text message alerts went off at the same time. His dad picked his phone from the table and read the screen. "Jarin is up next. We'd better get going." He took a drink from his smoothie and cringed. "What is this crap?"

"Mango." Bane smiled. "I thought that one would be the easiest to drink."

Dad pushed the cup away. "I'd hate to taste the worst. And on that note, let's go watch a competition based on the laziest thing a kid could possibly do all day."

His disgusted tone brought Bane's childhood memories back in technicolor surround sound. Obviously the apple hadn't fallen far from the tree, since he felt the exact same way about the tween's favorite pastime.

Chapter Twenty-Three

Jarin placed third in the video game competition. After hours on top of hours of nonstop noise and migraine-inducing colors, Dahl couldn't wait to get home.

While the big kids had decided to branch off and bug other parents for a change, Bane had had an emergency at work. Tasked with putting the little ones to bed, Dahl was getting deathly serious about her monster-trapping duties.

"This is ginger root — and monsters are repelled by the smell." Next to the cutest soon-to-be kindergartener ever, she lay on her stomach and studied the empty space underneath the bed. Dahl left the vegetable in the center of the floor.

"What happens if it doesn't work?" Cady whispered.

Missing the kid's number one monster slayer — who, strangely enough, was Alana — Cady had enlisted Dahl as what appeared to be a poor substitute. "What creature wants to go up against your Uncle Bane? He's the biggest, meanest monster killer I have ever met."

"Uncle Bane isn't scary." Cady giggled.

Dahl let down the bedskirt and sat up. "Monsters are very scared of Uncle Bane." She pulled back the blanket for the kid. With her siblings gone, Cady didn't have anyone to save her. Usually they tried to find one of her little friends to spend the night, but no one was available.

"If they come back, can I sleep with you, Dolly?" Cady crawled into her bed.

Hell no! She almost swore out loud. With the kid well on her way to millionaire status off that stupid swear jar, Dahl swallowed her initial words. "Trust me, sweetie. You won't need to." She pulled the covers up to Cady's chest and kissed her cheek. "That ginger will do the trick. They'll go to some other kid's house tonight."

"But if they do come back, can we get a dog?" Dahl already knew the answer to that one. However, Bane would have to deliver that blow.

"We'll see." She provided the patent non-answer. "Starry light?" The chubby-cheeked imp nodded. Dahl flipped the switch on her nightstand lamp that illuminated her ceiling. Pretty stars circled above them. "Night, butterfly."

"Goodnight, Dolly."

Dead tired, Dahl backed into the dim hallway. Suddenly swept off her feet, she found herself pinned against the wall, face-to-face with the slayer of monsters. Bane kissed her hard—a sweet, punishing kiss. He fought his way into her mouth with his tongue. Barely holding in a groan, she nipped his lowered lip.

"First," he panted, out of breath, as he ran his hand up her shirt, "she will *never* sleep in the bed with us."

He pecked her lips and pulled the top of her bra down to finger her nipple. "Second, we're full up on living, breathing tenants who don't pay bills. No dog."

"Objection," she muttered between kisses. Horny and tired made an iffy combination. Knocking out a good orgasm chased with a long, hot bath could possibly help the day end on a high note.

"Nope, putting my huge monster-slaying foot down."

"There's such a big age difference between the kids. I think Cady could use a…" At a loss for words, she melted to the feel of his lips on her neck.

Bane growled low in his throat. He lowered his head against her shoulder. Swiftly snaking his hand around her waist, Bane guided her down the hall toward the master bedroom. "One problem at a time, sweetheart." He flipped the light switch in the room and shut the door with his foot.

"If that's the attitude, we'll never accomplish—Oomph!" As he tossed her onto the bed, Dahl's words caught in her throat. When he yanked his shirt over his head, she admired his muscled abs. "What the hell happened to you?"

"Warner wanted to meet in person."

"That bad, huh?" Enjoying the show, she pushed herself onto her elbows and waited for him to take off more clothes.

"Oh yeah." Bane unbuttoned his jeans. "The last woman Shawn attacked isn't going for the payoff like his other victims. She wants to press charges."

"Let me guess." Dahl held up her hand to stop him. "The owner and coach believe this will blow over."

"And if it doesn't go away, you know who they'll blame." Pushing down his pants, he stepped out of his jeans and kicked them to the side. "Everything I worked for in the gutter... For what? A man I never wanted on the team in the first place." When he shoved his black briefs off, his huge cock sprang free.

"This Warner guy... How rich is he?" she asked. Dahl flipped onto her stomach and scooted around on the bed to face him.

"Why?" He smirked. "Are you looking to replace me?"

Gladiator hot, this man would have won every match. "Nah... Who wants to learn someone new?" she said, throwing his words back at him.

"Comforting," he grunted.

Signaling him with her finger to come closer, she flipped her hair back and smiled. "But I might have a plan."

Bane stepped in front of her in all his glorious nakedness. "Want to share?"

"Maybe later." Dahl reached for his rod and kissed the tip.

"Mm-m," he groaned.

Without more prompting, she opened her mouth to suck his cock.

The whole day had turned into a next level Willy Wonka film that included all the intense acid colors. The apology from his father had been unexpected. After Jarin had placed in his competition, Warner had called and requested they meet. The news about Shawn hadn't surprised him but had definitely put a damper on his good mood.

Bane had hoped that once he arrived home, Dahl would still be up. He'd wanted to work out his problems between her sexy legs. However, all thoughts seized once she positioned herself on the bed and gestured for him to come closer.

Snatch her clothes off and take her from behind.

But he needed to maintain control of the situation. In every aspect of his life, he had to be the authority, but Dahl Baby Hamilton had a way of breaking down each barrier.

She reached for him with a delightfully smutty smile then kissed the tip of his cock. Dahl teased the head, swirling her tongue around it before she deep-throated him.

"Oh fuck," he ground out. *This freaking woman will be the death of me.*

The other night he'd told her the truth—that he had always loved her. Now older and wiser, he had to wonder if he should trust her again.

She was the only woman who had the ability to crush him. Determined to relax, he pushed his cock farther into her mouth. Happy with a good blow job, Bane refused to let her gain the upper hand. She already controlled everything else.

As he rolled his hips to fuck her throat, Dahl sweetly cupped his balls. "Yeah, baby, yeah." He humped her mouth with deliberate thrusts, then picked up the pace. The added pressure of Dahl jiggling his balls sent him straight over the edge. "Arrgh," Bane moaned.

A rush of warmth spread through his soul before he squirted his seed down her talented throat.

Chapter Twenty-Four

A split-second decision brought him to the stadium. Bane needed to grab paperwork from his desk then head to court. They'd made a few more cuts to the team, but the bigger ones would come later. During the off season, regular staff toiled around the office. Not much happened in the early months. Everything picked up closer to the season opener.

"Unfortunately, when you have a high-profile career, there are people — more specifically women — who want to take advantage of that situation," Shawn said.

Bane turned toward the conference room. A camera crew spilled out into the hallway. He drew up short at the sight of the Mavericks' quarterback in the middle of a one-on-one interview with his second ex-wife, Rachel True. Lights were stationed around the humble-appearing all-American football player.

He stepped over the wires and went to the room next door. After Warner had given him the heads-up, Bane knew what would happen next. He walked into a nearby office where the owner and coach studied the monitors.

"My invitation to the snow job must have got lost in the mail." Bane leaned over the coach, who sat in front of the monitor.

"We needed to get in front of this," Coop said. He almost sounded contrite.

"By asking my ex-wife to conduct the interview?"

"The coach believed it showed unity," Coop replied.

Appearing twice as old as he did when Bane had last seen him, the old ass sat there with his cowboy hat in hand.

"Besides, Shawn's comfortable with her, and he needs to come across in a good light."

Figuring the coach had had enough of smelling his armpit, Bane stood up. "Yeah, because that sexual predator scent he wears is a problem."

"Now wait a minute." Before the coach could move from his seat, Bane shoved him back down.

"Don't get up, coach." He patted the man on the shoulder while nodding at the monitor. "I'm sure the show is almost over." Rachel hugged Shawn. Bane fully understood that once the DA buried the quarterback underneath a pile of evidence, the idiot's career was over — then Bane's would be next.

Mustering up his most affable smile, he stepped into the hall to greet Satan herself.

"Tell Todd that I want to be in the editing booth. There are a couple of shots we may need to cut. Bane, sweetheart!" she cooed. Skinny, bordering on runway thin, she made a beeline to him. Rachel had a strange Lena Horne type of beauty that leaned toward pristine. He had never seen her with one hair out of place.

"Rachel…" Bane bent down for his extremely polished ex-wife to kiss him on the cheek. "How are you?" He allowed her well-maintained façade to play out in front of everyone. Since it took less than five minutes for her to get on his nerves, he decided to allow her a maximum of three.

"Well—and yourself? I heard that little bartender is back in town?"

Unable to stop himself, he laughed. "World-renowned chef… But for the sake of your ego, we'll go with bartender."

As he guided her toward his office, she placed her well-manicured hand on his arm. "My ego? I don't know if this has escaped your notice, but I'm now lead anchor at the Celebrity Channel," Rachel told him.

"Strangely enough, it has." Bane waited until they made it into his office. "Why the hell did you take this interview?" he inquired pleasantly enough.

"They offered it."

He nodded. "One more nail in my coffin?"

"Not at all. I figured I'd help you out, show you I'm not as bad as you think I am." Running her hand through her sleek, chin-length bob, she provided him with a disingenuous grin.

"If the rumors about Shawn are true, this little 'R Kelly plead my case' doesn't help anyone."

"Hopefully"—she beamed with confidence—"you'll provide me an exclusive to why you kept a rapist on your team."

"Whoa." He held up his hands. "Who says it was me?"

"The coach." Rachel wandered around his office. "Coop. They both said, and I quote, 'Bane makes all hiring and firing decisions.'" She stopped at a picture on the wall of his brother with his family. "Sorry to hear about Devon, by the way."

"Yeah?" Bane tried to process the crap she had laid on him. "Thanks for the condolence card. Oh, that's right… You didn't send one."

"Well, I wanted to call, but…"

"Sure, I remember, you hate emotions." He picked up the files he had come to the office for.

"That's why we used to be such a great team! You don't like the warm, fuzzy stuff either." She practically crossed the room without a sound. "Come on, Bane. This doesn't have to be awkward." Rachel hitched her little body onto his desk and purred. The thing she had never understood was that her prettiness never translated to allure. Confidence and self-awareness made a woman sexy, not merely an attractive shell.

"Sorry, Rach, but the minute you contested our prenup, it got awkward."

"We all can't be satisfied with pennies, like that short fry-cook you shacked up with."

Ah-h-h. It suddenly dawned on him why she was so eager to bury his career. Word must have gotten back to her about Dahl. Together, he and Rachel had had a power-couple type of relationship that had garnered attention. Unfortunately, the thing she could never get enough of was the spotlight. They liked each other well enough, but that was where it had ended. Bane had realized a little too late that he didn't want that type of relationship for the long haul.

Bending close to her ear, he inhaled the sharp scent of freesia. That was something else about her he didn't miss. "She makes more money than me, so when this all goes to shit, I'm staying home with the kids."

Allergic to broke, Rachel quickly slipped off his desk and scooted toward the door at a quick clip. "That's sweet," she muttered, before straightening any perceived wrinkles out of her skintight dress. "My assistant will give you a call if we have any follow-up questions." She opened the door.

"Thanks for the heads-up," he said, pleasantly enough, to annoy her.

She snorted before she stepped out of his office, slamming the door shut. Not in the least bit pleased, he snatched his desk phone off the hook. After hitting speed dial, he waited for Warner to answer.

"Hey, man," he said once the sports agent picked up, "we've got a problem."

* * * *

Rain pelted the top of Dahl's umbrella as she waited outside her agent's office. Her agent was a hard-core shopaholic and Dahl knew which direction she would likely go after work.

Trish stepped out of the downtown building and headed toward the Water Tower. Slightly hindered by the high heels she'd worn for court, Dahl had to pick up her speed.

"Trish." Ignoring the pain, she doubled her steps to catch up. "Dammit, Trish, I know you hear me!"

The tiny woman whipped around. "Are you stalking me now?" she hissed. Since Dahl's heels allowed her a bigger height advantage than usual, she towered over the little fairy. To keep her agent dry, she shielded her with the umbrella.

"If you would take my calls, I wouldn't have to."

"Why the hell would I? You fired me!" she screamed. A couple of people glanced in their direction on the busy downtown street but no one really cared. Most Chicago natives were used to the occasional sporadic street argument. Hopefully, this one didn't end in an actual fight.

"Did the actual words 'you're fired' come out of my mouth? Because that honestly doesn't sound like me."

"Dammit, Dahl, you went behind my back and tried to push that stupid idea to other publishers." Trish shoved her black-framed glasses onto her button nose.

"In my defense, I gave you a heads-up, so it wasn't exactly behind your back. It was more dead ass in your face," Dahl admitted sheepishly.

"That makes it better?" Trish turned away from her and braved the wet Chicago streets without cover.

"Fine." Trish was pretty fast for a tiny chick, so Dahl ran to catch up. "I'm sorry." She grabbed Trish's arm and forced her to stop. "This is the first time in my career that I have failed on every level and I don't know how to handle it. I needed someone to blame and I'm sorry I picked you."

"It hurt my feelings." Trish pouted.

Way to shove that knife in deeper. Dahl frowned. "That was not my intention." Uncomfortable with all this lovey-dovey mess, she shifted her weight from foot to foot. In retrospect, heels really weren't her thing, no matter how sexy they made her look.

"Fine. But if you do it again, you won't have to worry about firing me—because I'll quit."

"Promise." Dahl nudged Trish with her shoulder and walked with her toward the high-end mall.

"Want to go shopping? Macy's is having a sale and I have a coupon," Trish sang. Shopping always made the little psycho happy.

"No can do. I have an appointment and I'm running late. I just wanted to hunt you down, beg for your forgiveness and ask for a favor."

"What made you think I'd let this go?" Trish asked.

"That's simple, my dear. I'm your favorite." The women stopped at a light, waiting to cross the street. "Also, can you loan me a couple of your clients for cooking lessons and launch parties? For their book release week, not mine — because apparently appetizers suck."

"No, don't tell me," Trish moaned. "You're still screwing with that stupid restaurant?"

"No, I bought it."

"Shit!" Trish hollered. Passing pedestrians stared at them. Losing momentum, Dahl hurried her agent across the street since she didn't have time to truly plead her case. "But I could have sworn I told you to dump that mess."

"Under new management. In other words, we're closed for a few weeks, then we'll come back bigger and stronger. That's why I need bodies to — "

"No snow job necessary, but I promise you're going to owe me big."

"Real big," Dahl promised. They stopped in front of the Water Tower.

"So where are you going, looking so hot?"

Delighted with the compliment, Dahl posed with the umbrella. "Wha-a? You think I look hot?" A couple of cars on Michigan Ave honked at her and she threw them a cheeky wave. "Court." She clutched her fake pearls and laughed.

"Whoever you killed, I'm sure the judge will let you off." They fist-bumped each other. "I'll see who I can dig up and give you a call."

"Trish, you're the best."

"Don't I know it," Trish said.

Officially tackling everything on her to-do list one hard task at a time, Dahl waited for Trish to step into the revolving doors. As soon as her agent was out of sight, she turned toward the street and hailed a cab.

Chapter Twenty-Five

Déjà vu washed over Bane as he corralled all the kids to make another trek down to the courthouse.

"Are you sure Dahl's coming? You know how you two get."

"Uh, she's never ghosted me before. Usually she tells me she's leaving..." Bane dumped everything out of his pockets and put it in the bowl at the security check point.

"Well, you're pretty hardheaded most of the time, and she's generally right when she calls you on your crap, so-o... Also, you took one hit too many," his dad rambled. "And don't forget that whole thing with your swimmers. I'm pretty sure you didn't tell her about those being fried."

"Are we going swimming?" Cady asked.

"No, sweetie. I was talking about your Uncle's jun—"

"Is this supposed to be a morale booster?" Bane cut the old man off. He had forgotten about his dad's lack of a filter. "Because I got to tell you... It's not working.

Besides, you wanted to help." They stepped through the metal detector.

"Well, I meant normal grandpa stuff like ice cream, not court."

"Are we getting ice cream after this?" Cady chimed in again. While his dad held on to the little girl's hand, Bane carried the baby in the carrier.

"Maybe... I sure could use some after this. What do you say, Bane? Ice cream?"

He scooped his stuff up from security and waited for his dad. It took the old man several tries to get through the machine. After what felt like forever, he finally wrangled all the loose change back into his pocket, and they headed to the courtroom.

"What has gotten into you?" His dad was downright twitchy, and this was the second time Bane had seen him nervous. *What the hell is with this man's medication?*

"Family court," his dad grumbled. "I hate court." Bane had nearly forgotten how many times his mother's side had filed for custody of him and Devon. That last time, around the age of thirteen, Dad had barely eked by with full custody. Considering Bane had done most of the heavy lifting growing up, he often wondered what his childhood would have been like if his aunts on his mother's side had actually won.

As the Carter name was called, they stepped into court before the doors closed.

"All rise." The judge walked into the room and took her seat on the bench.

"Good to see you again."

"Judge, the Carters had another incident. I believe it is imperative that we remove the children as soon as possible," the opposing lawyer started before anyone else could talk.

Bane opened his mouth, but his attorney placed a hand on his arm and shook his head.

"Mr. Hill, where are your clients?" the judge asked.

"Well, I...uh... It was such last-minute notice that they weren't able to get away. He has his own children and business, so he would need a lot more lead-time than—"

"That's what I thought. Custody will remain with Bane Carter." The judge picked up her gavel to bang it.

"Hold on! What about DCFS or the break-in at the Carter household? There's no way these children are secure in his care."

"The DCFS agent submitted her report, and the Carter household was deemed safe. After speaking with the detective about the fire and the break-in, he also considers the Carter household safe. His words, to be exact, were 'safer than the Cleavers'."

"Who?" Alana asked.

"Young lady, don't tell me you've never seen Nick at Nite?" the judge responded in disgust.

"Nick at what?" Cady tugged at Bane's sleeve.

"If there's nothing further." She held up her gavel.

"But the latest incident at the Carter household shows—"

"Counsel, it's an ongoing investigation. I'm sure if you have any information, the detective would love to hear from you." She banged her gavel. "Mr. Carter, please join me in my chamber."

"Can we get ice cream now?" Cady whined. The fact that she had kept quiet that long was purely amazing.

"What's going on? Are they going to arrest you?" Alana's voice went up a notch.

"Your Honor, should I join you?" Bane's attorney asked.

The judged waved his attorney away. "Just Mr. Carter."

"All rise," the bailiff said. Everyone stood for the judge to leave the bench.

"Uncle Bane—"

"Give me a sec, sweetie."

"What's going on?" his dad asked. All eyes were on him. He merely shrugged and followed the judge out of the door to her chambers.

As he stepped into the drab civil office, his eyes were immediately drawn to Dahl. She stood in the middle of the stuffy room, dressed in a form-fitting cream dress. Her bouncy curls were styled in in a sexy peekaboo swoop. Hard-pressed not to grin like a five-year-old on Christmas morning, he couldn't help himself.

"Did you want your family here for this?" the judge asked. She stationed herself in front of her desk.

His ex-wife was even more beautiful than the day he'd laid eyes on her at some stupid award ceremony. When he'd seen her, Bane had nearly dropped his plate of food. From afar, he'd shadowed her throughout the night, waiting for his chance, and the minute he'd found a clear shot, he'd pounced. Laying it on thick, he'd managed to get her number. Bane wished he had known at twenty-one what he now knew at forty-one— then he would have never let her go.

Slipping his arm around her waist, he took her beautiful, full lips to his.

"Ahem." The judge interrupted his musing.

"Sorry," he apologized.

"Are you sure you don't want everyone here for this?" Dahl asked. Later he had plans for her and everything curvy underneath her dress.

"No… Just us," he told her.

Dahl nodded with a smile.

"Okay then," the judge began. "Winston Bane Carter, do you take this woman to be —"

* * * *

The downtown loop had all the good clubs — jazz, electro and blues to name a few. Not entirely sure how to go about her special recon mission, Dahl dragged Trish along.

While Dahl typed away on her phone, her agent eyeballed the big bouncer who headed the line in front of the burlesque club's door.

"Uh, you promised me dinner for being such a dick." They stood to the side of the long line of people who waited for entry into the club.

"This will only take a minute —"

"Then you went and got married without inviting me," Trish continued. "By the way, for the record, the only reason I'm here on date night is that my plans fell through."

"Um, what's with the 'tude?" Dahl asked.

"I just thought we were bigger than this."

Dahl glanced away from her phone and took in Trish's round, pouty face.

"Oh, hey now. What we did was a super-fast, off-the-cuff decision. Don't be offended, sunshine." She rubbed the little pixie's shoulder and went back to texting dinner instructions to Alana. All the girl had to do was reheat a freakin' lasagna. *How hard is that?*

"Oh God, not you!"

"Is that any way to greet your cousin?" Dahl schooled her face into a non-judgey expression. Considering that Melanie was wearing a Tina Turner jean outfit from the eighties—except whorier, if that were possible—the task had been difficult. "Uh, is this theme night?"

"Every night is theme night," Melanie sighed. Joining them against the wall, she slipped off her ridiculous high heels to rub the arch of her foot.

"Why Tina? You're more of a Whitney Houston."

"One of the veterans called dibs. You didn't trek downtown to talk eighties glam. What do you want?"

"Now, now, be sweet," Dahl admonished her. "We come in peace."

"Don't look at me." Trish snorted. "I'm only here for the food."

"Our breaks are short. What's up?" Melanie's tone lightened a smidge—but not by much.

"What's this place...a strip club?" Dahl nodded at the bright neon sign next to the feathered dancer at the entrance.

"Different stages of nudity, but the owners wanted to keep it classy. Lots of old-timey stuff. You know, Gypsy Rose Lee crap." She finished with one foot then switched to the other. "On the upper floors, there's a little boob stuff, but nothing more than that." Dahl lifted her eyebrow but held her tongue. "I'm in the Internet department. I go over the basics and train the newbies."

"Do you have any rich regulars? I'm looking for a kid from a wealthy family," Dahl said.

"Sure, we have a few of them, but they come for the fancy décor."

"Tits." Trish pointed at Melanie's breasts with a smirk. "They're really here for the tits."

"Tell me about it," Melanie agreed. "You'd think these could solve all the world's problems."

"These guys have a preference?" Dahl continued, completely ignoring them.

"Yeah, they all do. What's this about?" she asked, fluffing her spiky blondish-brown wig.

"We have an event tomorrow—a small, intimate affair. If these rich guys' favorite performers can bring them, I'll have a hundred dollars and a free meal waiting."

"And me... What's in it for me?"

Dahl took a step forward and placed her face directly in front of her cousin's. "Not going to jail for fucking fraud... That's what's in it for you."

They stared each other down until Melanie moved away from her. "Fine... But for the record, the little bit of money I got from the restaurant was only enough to get me caught up on my mortgage payments."

"Cool, because I hear those cots in the pen suck." Dahl couldn't resist taking one more swipe at the ingrate.

"Mel, let's go!" A stumpy Danny DeVito impersonator stood in the door. "We're a bottle girl down and the newbies have a short attention span."

"Time's up." Melanie plumped her breasts inside of the tacky, lacy bustier. "I'll talk to the twins, Burgundy and Wine, and see what I can do."

"Be convincing."

"Hey, wait up," Trish called after Melanie. "How much do bottle girls make in this joint?"

"Commission."

"What do they have to wear?"

"Slutty Disney costumes," Melanie told her.

Trish glanced over her shoulder. "Well..."

"Well what? We have reservations at that new place up the street."

"I'll give you a free pass for the next time you mess up, if you let me do this."

Dahl wanted to complain, but the offer was too good to pass up. Odds were, she would do something even worse the next time. "Fine, but I want pictures."

Trish squealed. "Do you think your boss will hire me? I waitressed in college."

"Aren't you an agent or something?" Melanie asked her on their way into the club.

"Yeah, but Tinder is a race to the bottom. Have you got a Snow White costume available? I think I can pull that one off."

Since Dahl's girls' night out had turned to shit in a matter of minutes, she texted Alana not to bother with the instructions.

Chapter Twenty-Six

Contemporary jazz played over the sound system in First Down. While servers passed around hors d'oeuvres to a room full of industry insiders, Bane stood by the bar and ordered a drink.

Dahl had made enough changes to the restaurant that it fit a sports-themed eatery better than the previous incarnation of First Down. Two walls were covered with oil portraits of all the Chicago greats, and the rest held huge high-definition televisions.

Some of the more unnecessary decorations had been switched out for a less formal feel. There were no more cream-colored fabrics and shiny wood. The change in décor made one heck of an inviting difference.

"Congratulations are in order, I hear," Warner said.

After Bane had married Dahl again, they'd taken the kids out for ice cream and broken the news. The Carter squad had appeared momentarily annoyed that they hadn't been able to participate in the ceremony. Dahl had promised them they could arrange the reception, which had thankfully quieted any future complaints.

Bane raised two fingers at the bartender. "Word gets around fast."

"Especially when you re-marry the first wife. That's good stuff, my friend." The bartender poured the restaurant's best bourbon and set the drinks down in front of them.

"Does Dahl have any family I can hit on?" Warner pushed.

"Yes, and when I say they're not cut from the same cloth, believe me on that." He chuckled. Melanie and Dahl couldn't have been more different.

"Dammit, why do the good ones always marry the grouchiest bastards?"

As his wife flitted from one guest to another, Bane tracked her movements from across the room. Two young guys with what looked like hookers on their arms shook Dahl's hand. Bane made a note to check out who the heck they were later. He picked up his glass and swallowed the dark liquid. "Think this is going to work?" he asked the agent.

"The only thing I know better than sports is rich people." Born of wealth, Warner had gotten himself disinherited ages ago. Considering that the smooth-talking man owned the number one sports firm, Bane figured he'd done okay for himself. "Trust me. It'll go off without a hitch."

Bane nodded in agreement before he finished the rest of his drink. After setting down the glass on the bar, he headed to the center of the main dining hall.

"Hey, everyone, thanks for coming." He waited to gain the room's attention before he continued. "At one point, the Mavericks were the top team in the league.

Unfortunately, that is no longer the case. Bad management and in-fighting among the players has plummeted the team's rankings. This is a new era, but old ideals are placing the Mavericks in a hopeless position. What I'm proposing to this room full of business-minded people is that we all pool our money and invest in a new legacy."

A gold lasso spun into a star on the screens behind him. The logo for North Rangers exploded.

"There's a non-compete for each city," the owner of one of the minor league baseball teams brought up.

"Those rules were changed last year, Norm. Let's not forget about the morality violations that are stacking up from all Shawn Mathers' crap—"

"You'll still need the votes from all the owners in the league."

"I'm almost positive we'll get them," Warner chimed in. "Come on, everyone. What do you say to new blood?" The agent held up his glass of liquor. Seconds ticked by, but less than a beat later, the people in the room followed Warner's lead.

"New blood!" they cheered with a toast.

* * * *

Four weeks had passed since they'd proposed buying the team. Two weeks before, the Mavericks had held football camp, and in less than one week, the team would celebrate their season opener.

Dahl went down the spiral staircase and passed the theater. When she opened the door to the workout room, beats from DMX poured into the hallway. It was knocking on three a.m. and neither she nor Bane could sleep. Tomorrow was Fan Appreciation Day, where their big move would be announced to a full house.

Bane was seated on the edge of the workout bench lifting free weights, sweat dripping down his huge muscles. *Damn this man.* Dahl's insides stirred at the sight of him. He finished his last rep and threw her a lopsided smirk. "This one's new?" Bane said, eying her outfit.

Amused that Bane loved her lingerie fetish, Dahl put her foot between his legs on the bench. Wearing a vintage number, she shifted her hip for him to see her lack of panties with the silk polka-dot baby-doll nightie.

"Sweaty," he told her.

"It's a good thing we have working showers. Worried?"

He set down the weight, ran his hand up her calf and kissed her knee. "Should I be?"

"Tomorrow may not go as planned," she said.

"Nothing ever does." He slipped his hand up the back of her thigh. "There's something I want to confess." Dahl quirked her eyebrow and leaned farther into his muscled body. "I've worked really hard on my career, and if it all ends tomorrow" — Bane lowered his chin to the top of her knee — "I'm good with that."

"Where is this coming from?"

"It kind of careens into my confession to you."

Dahl tilted her head to the side and waited.

"I have a low sperm count, and the odds of me having my own kids is almost" — he lowered his eyes and kissed the top of her knee — "nil."

"What did you say?" Dahl dropped her foot and took a step back as his confession slowly sank in. "Oh shit."

"There's nothing to suggest that playing football was the cause—" he hurriedly explained.

"And you didn't think to mention this when I was pouring out my guts—or even before we got married?" Not pissed in the slightest since she absolutely knew his motive, Dahl patiently waited for his reply.

"Baby, you were upset. I didn't want to burden you with my crap." He snaked his hand out and snatched her around the waist. She landed on his lap. "Hold on. Let me finish before you do that thing that you're dying to do."

"What thing?" She smirked.

"Gloat."

"Okay, but make it quick."

"Let's look at this logically," Bane half laughed and groaned. "I have inherited four monsters who have tripled my electric bill, keep clogging my toilets with God-knows-what and eat their weight in food. On top of all that, I've remarried the woman I should have never let walk out of my life in the first place."

Against her will, Dahl felt her insides soften. Slipping his fingers through the curls on the back of her head, he kissed her neck.

"Regardless of what happens tomorrow, I love you and everything about my life. Now go ahead and say it... 'I told you so'."

"Winston Bane Carter, if you think it's going to be that easy, you're cra—"

Smashing his lips into hers, he cut off her smart-ass reply. He inched the silk fabric past her breast and pulled her nipple into a tight bud.

"Mm-m," she moaned. Bane was evidently on a mission to fuck her into a stage of amnesia. Dahl decided to let him try.

Chapter Twenty-Seven

Fan Appreciation Day had everything from food to players, but not any actual football game. While team introductions were made, food vendors set out their latest concoctions. Different games for the kids were placed around the stadium, and the festivities would end with a sleek video presentation of the team's history.

After all that fun, fun and more fun, Coop would take the opportunity to tell the crowd how none of it could be possible without the fans. Then Bane would speak before the players would sign autographs to one hundred lucky winners of whatever contest had brought them to the stadium that day.

Dahl wove her way with the kids through the throngs of people in the parking lot.

"Watch it, Alana," she warned the selfie-snapping freak before she got stampeded by a group of boys.

"Are you okay?" A dead ringer for the teen Justin Bieber—not the seventies-style porno one—snatched her out of the way.

"Um, uh, y-yeah," Alana stammered.

"Nick." He smiled.

"Hey, you go to Oak Brook Academy?" Dahl took in his jacket.

"Yeah. I'm transferring this year."

"That's where Alana goes."

"Dahl," the girl hissed at her while self-consciously tucking a stray curl behind her ear.

"So where are you sitting?" Dahl asked.

"Uh, nosebleeds. My dad won tickets through his job." He hitched a thumb at the kids who were ogling the ice cream truck's menu in the parking lot. "I'm stuck with my little cousins."

"We have a booth." Dahl hurried to hand him a pass. "Bring everyone."

"No way? Cool." He dashed off to meet with his family.

"Dahl!"

"What?" She headed toward the entrance. "He's new in school and on the basketball team. Didn't I tell you to make new friends?" They stepped into the entrance. "And he's cute."

"Yeah, he is."

"Lana's got a boyfriend," Cady sang with the accompaniment of kissy faces.

"Don't be a pain, sweetie. Alana has the power to help you or leave you to the wolves when you get older."

"Thanks, Dahl," Alana said as she snuck a peek over her shoulder at the boy.

Dahl sincerely hoped Bane didn't crush the kid's soul. She could tell what his plan had been by the moony look that had entered his eyes the minute he'd caught sight of Alana. Who knew what the little sweetheart would have done once he tried that *accidental* bump trick at school?

"Hey, stranger." Jeff, the producer, waved. He had two kids and his wife in tow.

Too busy to work on a pitch for a show, she'd sent him a few tickets to the Mavericks' Fan Appreciation Day to make it up to him. "Glad you could come."

"Me too. I wanted to get out before we geared up for our new show."

"Huh?" Although she had no idea what the hell he was talking about, she matched his huge smile.

"The videos with you and Cady. I used them for a pitch, and the network gave us the go ahead. I figured we can get a few other chefs with their kids and crank it out for mid-season replacements."

"No sh-h—" Dahl caught herself. *Stupid swear jar.* "Snakes." She threw the kids a wink before she continued on. "They liked it?"

"Loved it." A horn blared, signaling the fans to take their seats. Jeff ushered his family into the stadium ahead of them. "We'll meet up soon to talk about it, yeah?"

Stunned at how simple that had turned out, Dahl hurried everyone to the executive elevator. They jumped into the cab and went up. She had twenty minutes to change out of her jeans and tank. After the hall of famers, Coop would introduce Bane.

The elevator opened to wall-to-wall people who occupied the executive floor. Press, former players and their guests mingled around the VIP area of the stadium.

Dahl waved at her agent. Trish was sipping on a fruity drink and dancing with her sister to the music piped into the room. She was either half drunk, kind of drunk or well on her way, but Dahl couldn't tell for sure. Dahl attempted to maneuver them around the packed house, glad Trish was taking the time to let her hair down.

"Oh wow, Lala... You've become such a beautiful young lady." Bane's stick-thin ex-wife pounced on them faster than a *28 Days Later* zombie. Alana stiffened underneath the hand Rachel laid against her back.

"And you, Sady... Look at you." When she addressed the little girl, the predatory leer never left her pretty face. Dahl glanced down in enough time to catch Cady rolling her eyes.

"Grandpa and Ms. Ester, Dolly." Not acknowledging the woman in the slightest, the little girl hopped from foot to foot, pointing to the leather recliners Ester had bogarted for her church friends.

"Go ahead," Dahl told her. While Cady zipped toward her two favorite people, Alana damn near melted into her side.

"Those little videos you make are darling. What do you say to an interview?" The entertainment reporter covered the side of her mouth and lowered her voice. "I'm sure Auntie Rachel can score you a spot on our new web show."

"Uh, I don't know...think, um..." Alana stuttered. "Dahl, I'm going to..." Moving faster than Dahl had ever seen, Alana zipped across the room to join her sister.

"Bane would be the one for you to ask about the interview, but you already know that, don't you?"

The fake happy act slipped off Rachel's face. "Well, Dahl... It's Dahl, right? I know a lot of things. For example, Bane's bid requesting a new team got shot down by the rest of the franchise owners. But that's a secret, so don't tell anyone." The woman placed her right hand on her hip and slowly pushed her hair out of her face, showing off her shiny engagement ring.

Ah, poor dude. Dahl smirked.

"I guess you'll be supporting Bane and all those kids on a baker's salary. You know, time to make the donuts." Rachel chuckled at her lame joke before placing her hand on Dahl's shoulder.

Behind the wench, Trish made a fist and pointed at Bane's ex. Feisty and possibly a wee bit crazy, her agent could take on the trash reporter. Quickly shaking her head, Dahl hoped the little nut got the hint not to tackle Bane's failed experiment, 'the not-Dahl'.

Rachel said, "Before he started working for the Mavericks, Bane got this awesome deal at ESPN. Too bad he had to go and epically crash and burn what could have been a lucrative career. Better you than me, sweetie."

"Not everyone is built for this type of scrutiny." Dahl dismissively flicked Rachel's hand off of her and smiled sweetly. "Let me know if you need better seats for the ceremony."

Rachel's eyes darted around the room, probably in hopes that they had an audience. "Wow, not too swift, huh? No worries. When it's all said and done, maybe you and Bane can give me an exclusive." She winked. "Besides, you do know the camera adds ten pounds, don't you? I mean, you really shouldn't be that close to the stage, in that case."

Dahl leaned toward the idiot for dramatic effect, since she didn't care who overheard them. "They're called tits—and you should buy some." Dahl walked away from Bane's pathetic ex-wife and sought out the Carter gang.

"Thought I was going to have to break up a fight," Bane's dad said with a chuckle as Dahl reached over to pluck a chocolate-covered strawberry off the bar.

"Nah, that would have been a rescue mission, Pops." She chewed the sweet treat and moaned.

"Don't forget our bet. I told you Rachel's silly behind would be slinking around. You owe me a cake," Ester said.

"Shame on you, Ester. I don't make fools' bets. If you want a cake, all you have to do is ask."

"Can I have a cake?" the woman kindly requested.

"Pie, maybe—and that's if you're good," Dahl told the old lady shyster. "Well, I have to get dressed." Already late meeting Bane, she needed to get a move on. She hurried toward the door, grabbing Alana by her shoulder.

"What was all that about with Rachel?"

"When we were kids," the girl began. Dahl arched her eyebrow but decided not to belabor the point that she was still a freaking kid. "Jarin jumped on her lap for story time and she shoved him off."

"Why am I not surprised?" Dahl groaned.

"She told the adults that he'd fallen and they believed her. Well, everyone but Bane." Dahl turned Alana around to face her.

"That sucks," she admitted. "But if I knocked Jarin to the floor, I would've made sure no one was watching." Alana laughed at her stupid joke. Since the kid didn't need any reminders of bad crap, Dahl decided to lighten the mood.

"It really doesn't matter anymore," the girl said, "because you're my auntie now."

"Rig-gh-ht." They slapped hands and exploded fists before Dahl nodded across the room. "Teen heartthrob just walked in. Go talk to him. But don't stand too close because Bane will crush his head in." Dahl shoved her in the cute boy's direction.

Officially late, she flashed her ID badge at security, who opened the door for her to dash down the stairway.

Chapter Twenty-Eight

Bane waited in the team's old locker room for Dahl. Basic in every way, it didn't have the latest flat-screens TVs or massage chairs. Coop had felt it was antiquated. The owner had pimped out the clubhouse to impress the reporters for after-game interviews. Despite their shoddy training equipment, Coop wanted the world to think that he spared no expense on his players.

The door opened from the executive stairwell and Dahl appeared, sexy and out of breath.

"Late." He tapped the face of his watch. "Why do you need to change your outfit? This one is family friendly."

"Which is not the look I'm going for." Dahl jerked her tank-top over her head, revealing one of those beautiful, old-timey corset thingamajigs underneath. She quickly popped open the button of her jeans and shimmied them over her waist.

Caught off guard, he stared at her wonderful, huge breasts, complemented by those full hips. Dahl kicked off her gym shoes then bent down and slipped her high heels on. The move allowed him a glimpse of her perfect bubble ass with no underwear.

Her little peep show put him in raging boner territory. Bane started to strip. Since he hated to give his speech in wrinkled clothes, he took off his sports jacket.

"Hold on. I thought we were running late," Dahl asked when she noticed what he was doing.

"Baby, you know I'm always up for a challenge." Bane worked the clasp to his watch to take it off. "What's off limits?"

Her smile brightened her whole face. "Alana's got my face beat, so no touchy lips."

Confused, he tilted his head. "What?"

"Makeup," she offered.

"Okay-y-y." He drew out his words. "What else?"

"The hair." She pointed at her curly updo. "This comes down into awesome waves, so no touchy there either."

Slightly disappointed that he couldn't grab a fistful of her gorgeous tresses, he groaned.

When Dahl unzipped the cup on her corset, unleashing her teardrop breast, Bane hissed. With a lopsided smirk, she slowly undid the next one.

"So no kissing and no hair grabs. Anything else?" He undid his pants to fist his rock-hard cock. Stroking his length, he approached her. "Turn around, baby." She swiveled slowly in her heels and placed her hands on the lockers to steady herself. Bane slapped her ass to admire the sexy jiggle.

Dahl gasped with a shudder.

Licking two of his fingers, he reached down to caress her pussy. "Oh-h," Dahl moaned underneath his touch.

She was already wet, and he thumbed her clit and tweaked her nub.

During his years in the league, he'd sought that high on the field. Now, the only thing that could match the rush was good sex. Seeking solace in the home of her hot body, Bane shoved into her folds. Dahl's pussy gripped his cock and squeezed him tight.

Placing his hand on the small of her back, he thrust into her, taking his time. If he could bottle their chemistry and sell it, he would definitely be able to quit his job from all the money he would make. With a slow stroke, he drew his cock in and out of her tight pussy.

When he nipped her shoulder, Dahl arched her back and pushed against him.

"Faster," she hissed. Racing against the clock, he wrapped his arm around her hip and rubbed her clit. "Oh shit, Bane!"

Too far gone, he forgot to warn her about the security guards who stood outside the door. The men were waiting to escort them onto the field. He opened his mouth to convey those thoughts, but only a strangled stream of gibberish fell out.

All the things he wanted to do to her would have to wait for later. He sped up his stroke. Before he let go into his wife's beyond-hot body, he grabbed her breasts and squeezed.

"That's right, baby. Fuck me!" Dahl taunted.

What kind of husband would I be if I can't follow simple instructions? Slamming into her pussy, he spurted a good stream of hot cum into Dahl.

* * * *

A sea of fans waited for the events of the day to begin. Once the front office finished yammering, the players would toss a few balls to the crowd. However, everyone's favorite was the shirt cannon. The stadium went nuts. T-shirts and jerseys were stuffed into five guns and launched into the stands. No one wanted to hear Coop prattle on, but they couldn't very well heckle the league's franchise owner.

Beyond relaxed from his quickie with Dahl, Bane stood off to the side of the stage. The coach introduced Coop, who waved to the crowd and made his way to the mic.

A funk of repulsive proportions wafted into Bane's nose and his brain short circuited. "What the hell, Jarin?" He peered down at the kid, who'd grown at least a foot over the summer. "You stink." Jarin was sweaty from playing go-fer for the team and Bane couldn't believe he smelled so bad.

"Our supervisor told me to skip the showers and come straight over here."

"There's no way you're getting in my car like that."

Jarin sniffed under his pit. "It's not that bad."

"Says the person not on the receiving end of that stench."

"Little Jaden, is that you?" Rachel strolled up to them. Her heels slowly sunk into the grass.

"Who? Do you mean *me*?" Jarin asked.

Rachel had barely had any real interest in Bane past his career status, which meant his family had never really made it onto her radar. Bane pushed the boy away, no longer wanting to be tortured by that teenage funk.

"Wow, they grow up so fast," his ex said.

"Rachel, I think I've seen you more in the past few months than in our entire marriage."

"Don't exaggerate, darling. It doesn't suit you." Regardless of the stadium full of people, Bane felt eyes on him. He took a glance around and found Rachel's camera crew off to the sides of the platform, giving him the once-over.

"Playing family with the wine taster... Cute." She nodded toward Dahl and the girls, who sat with the other executives. "Are you back with her because she didn't fight you on her crappy prenup?" She snorted at her joke. Rachel probably still found it hard to believe he hadn't wanted to hand over his pension to her on a silver platter.

"We didn't have one." He cleared his throat, fighting back the urge to laugh. Pretty sure she didn't know about his recent nuptials to Dahl, he waited to see what Rachel really wanted.

"Huh. Well," she replied, "good for you." Bane had recently come to understand where her animosity stemmed from. After Dahl, he had checked out. In some ways, he had to accept blame for the demise of his second and never-should-have-been marriage.

"Not that this isn't pleasant, but you do have enough pull at the stations to skip these little soundbites," he told her.

"Coop asked me personally." She sniffed. "Why would I turn down an invitation by the owner of the Mavericks?"

Bane tore his attention away from the stage to focus on her. As she ran her hand through her sleek haircut, she held her mouth in a twisted frown. She was usually better at schooling her features, so he wondered why she put herself in his path if she hated him so much.

"Nice ring." He nodded at the diamond on her finger. "Did he finally leave his wife for you?" Rachel's boss, who had joined the rest of her crew near the edge of the stage, glared hot hate in his direction. She had been hired at the Chicago office toward the end of their relationship, and Bane knew it would only be a matter of time before she'd sink her claws into her producer.

"It took a minute. It was a toxic relationship, after all."

"Believe me. I know all about those." He chuckled.

"Save those jokes for when you're out on your ass," Rachel hissed. "They didn't okay your franchise bid, and that white boy you trust so much? Yeah, Warner bought the Mavericks from under your nose. Oh, look! Here comes the moment I've been waiting for."

Coop held his arm out for Warner to join him on stage. Rachel's momentary confusion was obvious, since Warner was not on the schedule. She would likely think Coop had made an unexpected change to the line-up. Tepid applause worked its way around the stadium. The fans had grown bored of this presentation eons ago.

"In his negotiations with Warner" — she stepped into his line of vision — "the only thing Coop was adamant about was your immediate resignation." Her face scrunched into her familiar mask of hate. "I hope that waitress has enough to support the whole household, because this bullshit dream of yours is over, Bane. Nobody's going to touch you after this."

Rachel attempted to stomp away but the grass interfered with her exit. Instead, she hobbled back to the press section.

After that little showdown, he caught Dahl's eyes. She offered him a sweet smile and Cady blew him a kiss. He pretended to snatch the smooches from the air in the palm of his hand and held it to his heart. The little munchkin laughed hysterically.

Coop began, "We here at the Mavericks are all about tradition. I have faith that this young man will carry on with my vision and respect what we have built. Welcome your new owner, Warner James."

The announcement received lukewarm applause. Warner approached the microphone. "Thanks, Coop. I promise to do my best by chauffeuring in a new guard." Obviously comfortable in front of the large crowd, the agent straightened his tie and threw out a megawatt smile. "I like days of old and nostalgia like the next person, but for the Mavericks to compete in this industry, changes will need to be made. Whether it's players, front office or executives, we need to adapt. Unfortunately, people like me and Coop are part of the big machine—and a hell of a good-looking one, I might add."

Bane was pretty positive the agent would have to shut down his dating profiles after this. Laughter and applause covered his next few words.

"It's time for an overhaul. And with that said, please welcome Fast Ricky's little girl, chef extraordinaire and the Mavericks' real new owner, Dahl Hamilton."

As Warner helped Dahl onto the stage, the big screen's camera panned away from the coach's and Coop's stunned expressions.

"First, I have to ask," she said, once she got in front of the microphone. "Do you like my dress?" Dahl stepped back to show off the white and purple fitted Mavericks jersey. It hugged her sexy-ass curves.

The crowd roared.

She turned to give the crowd a shot of the extended logo. The stadium camera zoomed in tight. A silhouette of a cowboy who had a gun on his hip and a grip on a lasso in hand covered her back. Everyone went wild.

"I'm not much of a public speaker, so I won't keep you long. We have important business to attend to. In T-minus four minutes, we'll be shooting our brand-new jerseys into the crowd."

The intense energy that pushed teams to win electrified the air.

"We are all family." Dahl picked up where she left off. "From the fans, to the players and staff, we're in this battle together. To show you how serious I am about this family business, my husband and the Mavericks' former general manager, Bane Carter, is going to lay out plans for this year's winning season."

Bane jogged up the stairs to the stage. In a few quick steps, he reached Dahl and took her by the waist. "That freakin' dress," he whispered in her ear. "I can't wait to strip that shit off you."

Kissing her glossy lips, he smothered the laugh of the one who'd once gotten away and had thankfully come back again.

Epilogue

The Mavericks won their season opener in bad-ass fashion. Tied in the fourth quarter, ten seconds before overtime, they had scored. Dahl mingled with the press afterward and did her best to wear her Mavericks' owner's hat instead of harassing First Down's kitchen staff.

A meet-and-greet for the players had been set up with the press. Hopefully, the sports writers would play nice, although Dahl doubted it.

"This little whatchamacallit is superb." Warner popped one of her mini hot dogs into his mouth.

"See that, Trish?" Dahl elbowed her agent. "He loves the appetizers."

Trish quickly sucked down her Moscow mule and swiped at her mouth with the back of her hand. "By winter, that tailgating cookbook we're working on will be on the shelves. Enough with the stupid appetizers already."

As Warner chuckled, Dahl made eye contact with the server and nodded at Trish's empty glass. After a few more stiff ones, her overworked agent could turn back into that sweet fairy she adored and not this crazy woman who kept showing up.

"Hey, I didn't get chance to thank you," Dahl said.

"For what?" Warner leaned over the bar and snagged a slider off an unattended plate.

"Ewww, what the hell?" Dahl asked, not impressed with what Warner had done.

"This is Art's." He pointed at an older, chubby man who was arguing with the bartender. "He's editor for some okey-doke newspaper. Trust me. I'm saving his life. He had a heart scare or some shit. Go on... You were telling me that I'm awesome."

Shocked by his filthy-ass ways, she momentarily forgot the topic of conversation. "Oh yeah." Warner had helped them pull off the steal of a century. If it hadn't been for him, they wouldn't own the Mavericks. All the participants who had attended the franchise meeting had been handpicked by the sports agent. He'd known that if he didn't get the right people into the room, one of them would run to Coop and tattle.

When the official word, beyond the rumors, had gotten out about claims of sexual assault against the popular quarterback, Coop had had to lower his asking price. *A football team with no star player couldn't really be worth that much, could it?* Once Dahl and Bane had hit up everyone who had been interested, they'd used Warner's name to buy the Mavericks. Only after she'd begged, borrowed and leveraged everything she had to become the majority shareholder had Dahl and Bane officially become the first African-American owners of a team.

"Mm-m, this is so damn good. You should be a chef or something." She noted Warner's inability to take a compliment.

"What are you guys talking about?" Bane placed his hand on her hip and buried his nose in her hair. She'd changed conditioners last week and he acted as if he couldn't get enough of the fruity scent.

"If it weren't for your trusty sidekick here, we couldn't have pulled off this caper," Dahl said. "I was just thanking him."

"Whoa, I am not the Robin to his Batman." Warner snorted before he reached over the bar and took a wing from a reporter's plate.

"Is that your food, man?" Bane asked.

"Don't say another word." She placed her arm on his chest. They didn't need to go down that rabbit hole again.

"No thanks needed," Warner said. "As a partial owner, if we win just one Mega Bowl, I'm set up for life. Besides, Bane gave me the money to start up the agency, so I kind of owed him."

"Ah-h, are you sure you don't want to be Robin?" Dahl asked.

"Sorry to interrupt this really sappy moment," Trish piped in. She plucked a fry off Warner's stolen plate of food and popped it into her mouth. "But your new guy is hot as hell. I might have to start watching this shit. No offense, but is that sexy mutha single?" Shawn's replacement leaned against the wall, fiddling with his phone. He hadn't muttered more than two words to anyone the whole night.

"Uh-h, he's Canadian. That's all I know," Bane said, even though he knew a lot about the man he'd hired.

"No shit!" Trish said. "I've never banged a Canadian before."

Warner nearly choked on his chicken wing. Tiny but sure of herself, Trish had no qualms about sex. The love 'em and leave 'em elf made no bones about her appetites.

"Hey, Dre," Warner called the cocky running back over. "What's with your guy?" he asked, once he'd joined them. Dahl didn't miss the twinkle in Warner's eyes. She wondered what deal he'd made with Trish that he wanted to snag her a man.

Just then, the Mavericks' PR assistant took the stage and opened the floor for anyone to ask questions to their new QB Gavin Knox.

Their tiny group continued their conversation. They were far enough away where no one could hear them.

"Knox? What do you mean?"

"Is he in a serious relationship?" Bane asked. "Not that it matters… I just want a heads-up so we don't get into a Shawn Mathers type of mess."

"Shawn was knocking on serial killer's door, so I doubt Knox will meet those awesomely low expectations." Andre snorted.

"Now that you mention it," Trish said, "he did look like he was totally capable of a little Michael Myers slasher action."

While Bane squeezed Dahl's hip tighter, Warner and Trish giggled. Bane hated any and all things to do with Shawn Mathers.

"It would be funny if it weren't true," Andre muttered. "Anyway, about my boy, Knox." He nodded at the makeshift stage where the six-foot-six quarterback had stepped up to the microphone. Dahl could see his appeal—dark brown hair, piercing blue eyes, and his chiseled face seemed open and sweet. He looked like the exact opposite of their previous QB. "When we were in college, he would get pussy thrown at him left and right."

"Dre," Bane warned.

"What? I've heard Dahl say ten times worse. And this one" — he chucked his thumb in Trish's direction — "comes to poker nights, so-o…"

"Just finish the story," Bane scolded his football player.

"Well, he used to get a lot of the good stuff."

"Bet it all wasn't good." Dahl scrunched up her face in disgust.

"Right." Trish cackled, and Warner made the sound of a rim shot.

"Oh gawd!" Bane dropped his head back, pinching the bridge of his nose. It was a clear indicator that he was sure to blow at their low level of maturity. Suppressing a laugh, Dahl rolled her hand for Andre to wrap it up.

"Somewhere around senior year all that stopped. I mean came to a screeching halt, and I've never seen him with anyone again."

"Is he gay?" Trish sounded disappointed.

"Man, I don't give a shit, as long he gets me that ball so I can take it to the end zone. But to answer your question, I don't think so. I just think he's got a situation of sorts."

"Great." Bane groaned. "As long as I don't have another Shawn on my hands, I can deal with it."

"Nope, you don't." Andre backed away from their group. "But you've definitely got something great with Knox."

As the running back disappeared into the crowd, the group's attention focused back on the press conference with the quarterback.

"Do you really think you can fill the shoes of an All-American quarterback?" Art the reporter poked at Knox. "I mean, you're Canadian."

Their group quieted to hear his response.

"What's your name, dude?" Knox asked.

"Art Newman, *Winnetka Gazette*," the chubby man introduced himself proudly.

"Cool, cool... Look, Artie"—the pretty quarterback's eyes twinkled as he pinned the journalist with a mischievous smirk—"I've got a bad-ass arm, and I hit my mark over eighty-seven percent of the time. I want you to remember that when you're writing in that shitty little paper about how awesome my Canadian ass is."

While Knox moved on to the next journalist, everyone chuckled at his slick burn.

"Well, my dear"—Warner held out his arm for Trish, and Dahl's elfin agent accepted it—"we're going to have to find you someone else. And, Bane, I think your cousin just walked in."

As Trish and Warner stepped away, Dahl snapped her head toward the door. Trey strolled in with a fat grin and a chick who wasn't Melanie. "Why, the nerve of that shit." She snatched a dirty fork off the bar, hoping to give him rabies or hep C.

"Hey." Bane turned her around to face him, nudging her chin up with his finger. "Have I told you how much I love you today?"

Dahl peered into the pools of the gorgeous man's eyes. "A couple more times wouldn't hurt," she purred, instantly turning into putty in his arms.

"To tell you the truth, I owe that moronic idiot a thanks. We probably wouldn't be together again if it wasn't for him." Bane slid his hand down her arm.

Dahl held up her ringless left hand. "It's his fault I have to wait a year to get a new ring." The thought of it made her want to pick up a knife instead.

Bane's low and husky chuckle tickled her ear. "There's no way in hell you should have given the last one to him."

"Come on, baby...just two little pokey pokes with the fork?" Dahl begged, as Bane eased the utensil out of her grip.

"To say that I'm happy you're back is a gross understatement. I love you, Dahl Carter."

"I love you more, Bane Carter."

"That's not possible," he muttered against her lips before he kissed her.

Since the only thing that mattered was Bane, everything else melted away.

Want to see more from this author? Here's a taster for you to enjoy!

Spies R Us
Amber Malloy

Excerpt

Spring was directly around the corner, which would conclude the twins' first year of preschool.

Vann idled at the kids' school in the carpool lane at the kid's school. He waited for the kids with Dylan Hansen, his best friend, in the passenger seat. Dylan had been a one-time silent partner in Vann's environmental investment firm, Good and Green. However, after this last quarter, Vann had been able to buy him out.

"They're late," Vann said, checking the clock on the pickup's dashboard. The little ones always got released first.

"Why don't you go check on them? That group of women over there are gobbling me up with their eyes, and it's making me feel naked."

"What?"

Dylan nodded toward the housewife gang and joked. "Unlike you, I'm not damaged goods. A runaway wife and two kids. I, on the other hand, am a shiny nugget of gold." Dylan chuckled as he pointed at himself. "Single and divorced moms can sniff me out a mile away. I think it's a sixth sense they acquire the minute they sign their names on the divorce papers."

Vann didn't doubt what Dylan said. The women were oftentimes overly friendly. He always wondered if it had to do with his semi-single status, but on the other hand, someone baggage free like Dylan would be prime beef.

"If you'd just divorce Eden, then you too could be held in high regard, such as I am." Dylan ran his hand through his blond hair and polished his fingers on his shirt. Friends since college, they were often mistaken for brothers. Yet ever since Vann had let his hair grow past his shoulders, Dylan appeared the more desirable of the two.

The mandatory uniform at Vann's company ended with jeans and began with a T-shirt—preferably clean, but that requirement wasn't always met. Once he'd shed his jacket and tie, the fairer sex had begun to migrate toward men with a more grown-up look. Jobless or homeless seemed to be the popular opinion about his life. Apparently neither of those options qualified him as good husband material, though they still seemed to look at him hungrily.

"I'm going to wait the five years to declare her dead. I think it would be easier for the kids." He didn't like to talk about Eden, but he knew Dylan meant well. To avoid further conversation on the subject, he grabbed the door handle. "To save you from the throngs of your admirers, I'm going to get the kids."

"Hey, I didn't mean to bring down the mood. I just want better for you, man. It's been too long."

Vann nodded. "No harm done. Let me get the kids. Then we can celebrate your return to the Windy City in high style."

"Oh please, not Showbiz Pizza," Dylan moaned.

"Of course not. We're going to Dave and Buster's."

Ivy League stuffy, Dylan was a snob through and through. "I hate that fuc—"

He slammed the truck's door on his friend's complaints and took a spot in the patch of dried grass uncovered from the freshly melting snow.

With his Starbucks Grande latte in hand, he hoped none of the moms in his kid's class noticed him.

"Hi there, stranger! We haven't seen you in forever."

Crap! Fighting his instinct to run, he gave the yoga mom a lame smile and tried to place the peppy woman's face. At six foot two, he was nearly a foot taller than her. He had to outweigh her by at least seventy-five pounds.

"I'm uh…busy. Work." He choked on his coffee drink when she slugged him on the arm.

"Where have you being hiding, you silly goose?"

Head of his own company, and he couldn't believe one PTA mom made him this nervous. He attributed his uneasiness to the manic gleam that shone in her eyes every time they spoke.

After the first week of preschool, Vann had realized single moms were natural predators and he didn't stand a chance against them. From that point on, Marta'd had to pick up the kids. Unfortunately her chipped tooth had forced him out into the wild today. To say he was guarded was an understatement.

"We need a strong, strapping fella like yourself for the spring pageant."

"Well, my schedule is kind of full—"

"I won't take no for an answer," the aggressive woman pushed. "We're meeting at Mary's at four p.m." She gestured at a group of moms who waved back. "Why don't you join us?"

"I, uh… Oh! Hey, there's the boys! I'll see what I can do."

"You know where to find me," she hollered at his back before he could put a good distance between them.

A perky little blonde he had never seen before walked between his kids, holding their hands.

"Are you the twins' dad? I'm Tess, but the kids call me Ms. Tess."

Last Vann knew, the boys' teacher hadn't been this young or cute. It didn't pay to dodge the PTA, he figured. "What happened to Ms. Lori?"

"Her mother had a nasty fall. I'm here until she gets back."

"That's too bad."

Tess smiled sweetly at him as the silence turned awkward. Vann had been alone for some time and he didn't want to get categorized as one of those pervy dads. However, the tips of her nipples pushing against the fabric of her sweater were hard not to notice.

"So…uh, nice meeting you."

"Huh? Oh!" A flush of red crept up her neck. "Sorry. I wanted to tell you that Miles got upset in class today."

"Are you all right, buddy?" He glanced down at his shy twin, but the kid wouldn't look up from his little boots.

"Yeah, I don't know what happened. The class was sharing what their parents did for a living. It was so cute. Louis said you were a green giant." Tess touched his arm with a laugh. "And then when it was time for Miles to talk about his mom, he started to cry."

Vann felt bad. The more sensitive of his two kids, Miles always had a hard time with the no-mom thing.

"My company finds the funding for green start-ups." He tried to clarify the interworking of his three year old's mind. "And my wife is out of the picture." Used to questions about Eden, Vann kept his answer short.

No one wanted to hear that one day she'd taken the boys to the doctor with the nanny but she'd never come back, which was the new version of Dad went out for cigarettes.

Tess' smile slipped into that familiar expression of pity he'd come to expect, but her recovery was better than most. "Well, I certainly didn't think you were a giant, and your job explains the..." She nodded toward his clothes before her words quickly died in her throat. "Oh God! I'm sorry." When she covered her mouth, her blonde hair swung back and forth as she shook her head. "I'm such a goof."

"It's okay." He laughed at her reaction to his worn jeans, plaid shirt and vest. "My job mostly entails places with lots of dirt then coming home to roll around with two three-year-olds." He shrugged. "A suit doesn't make much sense."

"You're right. You're right and I'm sorry."

"No harm done." He laughed again, amused by her embarrassment.

"Hey, Dad," Louis said, interrupting them, "can we go?"

"Sure, sure."

"Well, I have to get back before the head hens scratch my eyes out."

Vann took a glimpse over his shoulder. The mom herd quickly turned away, pretending to be in a deep conversation.

"Single dad with all his teeth... Throw in a horn and just call me a unicorn," he joked. "Besides, you should probably get in there before you get any colder."

Tess followed his eyes down her sweater. The tinkle of her laughter told him she wasn't offended by his observation. "No wonder they're shooting daggers at me," she hiccupped. Vann found her innocence refreshing.

"I want you to take care, Miles," she told the three year old, patting the little boy's arm. "It was nice meeting you, Mr. Morgan." She opened the door and shyly smiled at him over her shoulder.

"Vann," he corrected her. "Call me Vann."

"Okay." She giggled once more before she went inside the school.

Vann guided them through the thick group of older kids who searched for their rides home. "So what do you guys think of your new teacher?"

"I like her," Louis told him. "You should ask her to come over to play."

"Miles?"

His only reply was a shrug. Vann wasn't sure how to interpret that. His older twin could be closed off more times than not.

"Let's go home and watch a movie." Vann ruffled Louis' curly head of hair. "Unless Miles is too upset?"

"I'm okay…"

"Me too," Louis said.

"Great, that means were all okay," he told his boys.

Home of Erotic Romance

Sign up for our newsletter and find out about all our romance book releases, eBook sales and promotions, sneak peeks and FREE romance books!

About the Author

Amber Malloy dreamed of being a double agent but couldn't pass the psyche evaluation. Crushed by despair that she couldn't legally shoot things, Amber pursued her second career choice as pastry chef. When she's not writing or whipping up a mean Snickers Cheesecake, she occasionally spies on her sommelier. Amber is convinced he's faking his French accent.

Amber loves to hear from readers. You can find her contact information, website details and author profile page at https://www.totallybound.com